Campus Bloodbath

Remo caught the girl just as she was falling face first onto the asphalt of the parking lot. She sank into his arms calling his name.

"What happened?" he asked.

"Blood," she answered. "Blood everywhere. I heard noises. I looked up . . . hit me in the face . . . wet, couldn't see. I wiped it off . . . felt ear, eye . . . blood . . . Doctor Wooley . . . dead . . ."

Remo moved outside, walking past huddled moaning shapes. This wasn't a dream. The students who saw these murders would never forget them; they wouldn't have to strap their heads to a television set to conjure up a fantasy of blood and death.

Remo turned to Chiun and asked, "Who did it?"

"I don't know," he replied, "but I'm going to find out. Let's go, we've got work to do . . ."

THE DESTROYER SERIES:

The Destroyer

SWEET DREAMS #25

by Richard Sapir & Warren Murphy

PINNACLE BOOKS   LOS ANGELES

THE DESTROYER: SWEET DREAMS

An original Pinnacle Books edition, published for the first time anywhere.

ISBN: 0-523-40901-X

First printing, October 1976
Second printing, September 1977
Third printing, April 1978
Fourth printing, February 1979
Fifth printing, November 1979

Cover illustration by Hector Garrido

Printed in the United States of America

PINNACLE BOOKS, INC.
2029 Century Park East
Los Angeles, California 90067

To Roscoe Pound who is as real as
anyone to the glorious House of Sinanju,
Post Office Box 1149, Pittsfield, Mass., 01201.

"Many men build dream castles. Only a fool tries to live in one."

—HOUSE OF SINANJU

Sweet Dreams

Chapter One

Anyone could die, but to die well, my dear, that was what he wanted.

Dr. William Westhead Wooley watched himself say these words on his 19-inch television screen. A drop of blood formed on the lips of his television image, first fuzzily, then in red clarity. The body lay across the floor of a well-lit laboratory. The president of the university was there on television, tears in his eyes. Other faculty members were there too, heads bowed.

"We never appreciated Dr. Wooley," said Lee (Woody) Woodward, director of college affairs. He choked back a sob. "We never really comprehended his genius. We treated him like just another physicist in a market glutted with physics doctorates."

Janet Hawley was there on the screen too, as blonde as ever, as pretty as ever, as buxom as

1

ever. In her anguish, she ripped a corner of her pale green blouse and just for a moment, William Westhead Wooley, dying, saw the rounded edge of a pink nipple above the sloping cloth of the nylon half-bra.

The Edgewood University faculty lost its sharp outlines, the television image faded, and bedroom walls began to replace suits and faces. The red blood on the lips melted away and the television image now showed Dr. Wooley on clean white sheets in a smoking jacket with a pad of paper, hearing a knock on the door.

The bedroom had several similarities to the one in which Dr. Wooley sat, with electrodes taped to his temples, their wires leading to the back of the 19-inch screen, set like a giant square eye atop plastic enclosed circuitry.

On the screen there was no frozen turkey dinner crusting in its cheap brown gravy, or yesterday's blue socks already filmed with dust. The windows were washed, mother's ferocious picture faced the wall, the floors were clean and the bed in the one-room apartment overlooking the vast muddy girth of the Mississippi from Richmond Heights, had, on the television screen, grown to double its size. But the greatest difference between the television image and Dr. William Westhead Wooley's room was Dr. Wooley himself.

Gone were the rutted remains of the pocked battlefield of juvenile acne. The skin was smooth, clear, and tanned. The nose was strong, as though crafted by a sculptor's chisel. Muscles appeared in the arms and the dimply pale puffed skin of the belly became flat with hidden muscle. Dark hair came upon the chest and the legs had a runner's spring. On television, Dr. Wooley was thirty-two and was writing his acceptance speech for the Nobel Prize when he heard the knock on the door.

On the TV screen, Janet Hawley came in, crying. What could she do? She had been threatened.

"Threatened?" asked the improved image of Dr. Wooley. He put a hand on her blouse. He unbuttoned the top button. The hand found the bra. It moved down toward the nipple. The bra came flying off and Dr. William Westhead Wooley proceeded to make passionate and glorious love to the wanting Janet Hawley.

There was a knock on the door. Dr. Wooley shook his head; he hadn't imagined that. The knock became louder.

"If you don't answer, I'm going to leave." It was a woman's voice. It was Janet Hawley.

Dr. Wooley carefully snapped off the electrodes and rolled the wires back to the set. He started to put on a pair of gray chinos rumpled on the bed. No, not the chinos, he thought. He threw the chinos into the closet, calling out:

"Coming. Coming. Just a minute."

He snapped a pair of light blue flare bottoms from a hanger. He snuggled into them. He pulled a yellow turtleneck over his head and began combing his hair even before his eyes were free of the yellow cloth.

"Willy, if you don't open this door, I'm leaving."

"Coming," he said. He bathed Canoe shave lotion across the splotchy face and dried the perfumey smell on his hair. Then with a big smile he opened the door.

"Zip up your fly," said Janet Hawley. "Why

3

aren't you dressed? The room is filthy. Do you expect me to wait here? I thought we were going out. It's bad enough I have to pick you up."

"Only because you never let me go to your apartment, dearest," said Dr. Wooley.

"The trouble with you, Willy, is that you always turn everything I say against me. We're talking about you."

Janet Hawley was exactly like her television image, blonde, fleshy, with a healthy lust about her body. Unlike the television picture, she was clothed up to her neck with a glaring yellow blouse, and almost to her ankles in a thick scratchy wool skirt.

"Take that yellow thing off," she said. "They'll think we're twins."

"Yes, dear," said Dr. Wooley. He hurled the yellow turtleneck off his body and into the closet with one smooth swing of his right arm.

"What is that?" yelled Janet Hawley. She pointed to the screen. She poked her head close to it. She looked at the nude blonde figure.

"That's me," she screamed. "And I'm undressed and I'm six pounds overweight. You've got dirty pictures of me and you're showing them on a tele--vision screen. Fatter than I am."

"No, dear, I'm not showing them. That's not a television picture. It is, but it isn't a television picture."

Janet squinted at the screen. It was her bad side, too. But the breasts seemed a little firmer than usual. Nicer in fact. But the strangest thing was that she was undressed with Willy.

"You made videotapes and did one of those

4

mechanical things to get you in the picture," she said.

"No, dear," said Dr. Wooley. He nervously rapped his knuckles together like palsied applause.

"Well, what is it? One of those secret devices for listening in on other people's affairs that are none of your business?"

William Westhead Wooley grinned, shaking his head.

"I'll give you a hint," he said.

"You'll tell me outright," she said.

"That's sort of hard. It's complicated."

"If you're calling me stupid, you'll never get your hands on one of these again," she said, poking a finger into the yellow bulge of her blouse, a purple lacquered fingernail that glistened.

"You're going to let me tonight then?" he asked.

"Not bare," said Janet.

"I wouldn't think of bare. But then again I did," he said and he explained.

The mind worked on signals, electric impulses. But they were different from the impulses of the television screen. The mind created images which a person saw in his imagination. Television created images taken from light waves or what was called reality. What his invention was able to do was to translate mental images into the electronic beams that ran television. Thus the tube was an ordinary television tube but instead of a station somewhere sending out signals, it was the mind that sent out signals, so you could watch what you were thinking.

He took her hand to the plastic enclosed cir-

5

cuitry. He put her hand on the clear plastic case. It felt warm to Janet.

"This is what makes it work. This is the translator."

He took her hand and put it on the electrodes.

"These attach to your head. They pick up the signals. Thus we have the signals from the mind into these, running along this, into this, which makes them into television signals and into the picture itself on the set. Dum de dum dum dum."

"You're not allowed to show dirty pictures on television," said Janet Hawley.

"You don't understand. We're not beaming these things through airwaves. It only goes on the wires in this room."

"They're dirty pictures," said Janet and that night she did not allow him more than a kiss on the cheek. She was thinking. This was a somewhat difficult exercise for Janet because it was a relatively new experience, and it so preoccupied her that William Westhead Wooley did not get to touch her bosom, bare or covered.

Not that her bosom remained untouched for the rest of that night. When she returned home to her apartment, her bosom was pinched, tweaked, slapped, and bitten by one Donald (Hooks) Basumo as her punishment for "wasting the night with that faggy teacher when I been here waiting for you. Whatta you two doing anyway?"

"I told you, dearest," Janet said, bending to pick up the five empty beer cans that littered the living-room floor. "I stay close to him because I think someday he may have some money."

"Yeah? How close are you staying is what I want to know?"

"Darling." Janet Hawley smiled. "Nothing. He never even touches me. He never even tries."

"He better not and you better not let 'im. I don't like my broads being handled by other people," explained Donald (Hooks) Basumo, displaying a morality based upon the fact that of twenty-seven arrests upon his record, a full one-third of them had failed to result in convictions.

Hooks emphasized this with a stinging right hand slap across Janet's bare breasts, then he sat back in a living-room chair and watched her clean the mess he had made in her apartment. When she finished sponging up the last of the spilled onion dip, Hooks pulled her into the bedroom and threw her onto the unmade bed where he raped her, Basumo's sexual technique bearing the same relationship to making love that the Blitzkrieg did to backgammon.

Then, still fully clothed, Hooks rolled off Janet onto his side and began to snore, the peaceful purr of the pure at heart. Janet Hawley undressed herself and lay in bed thinking.

An hour later, she kissed Hooks on the neck. He growled but snored on. A half-hour later, she tried again and this time, the snoring stopped.

"Honey," she said. "I've been thinking."

Hooks blinked himself into the waking world.

"Whadja say?"

"I've been thinking, honey," said Janet.

"Get outta here," said Hooks and belted her in the ear.

She screamed. She yelled that it was her apartment. That she paid the rent. She bought the beer. He had no right to hit her.

So he hit her again and now he was fully

awake. The screaming had done it. He told her he would listen to her if she brought him a beer.

She answered that she wouldn't bring him a beer if his face was on fire. He hit her in the other ear.

She brought him the beer and told him that all night she had been thinking about a marvelous device she had just seen. You could get thoughts on a television screen, see whatever you imagined. All you had to do was think something and you would see it acted out for you on TV.

"For this you woke me?" he said.

He didn't like the idea. Anything that required thought would not sell to the American public, he said. Things that sold to the American public were things you didn't have to think to use.

She said she had seen dirty pictures on the screen.

Hooks Basumo cocked his head.

"You say dirty?" he asked.

"Yeah. You can imagine yourself humping any-body."

"Yeah? Raquel Welch? Sophia Loren?"

"Yeah. Burt Reynolds. Robert Redford," she said.

"Yeah? Charo? Maude's daughter?"

"Yeah," she said. "Clint Eastwood. Paul Newman. Charles Bronson. Anybody."

He belted her again because she seemed able to think of more names than he could, but then he stayed awake the whole night, making Janet tell him all the details, making sure she didn't forget anything. What he heard was money, lots of money.

And when he described it to a local fence the

next day, he said he knew where he could get his hands on a new kind of porno machine. Anything you imagined would appear on the screen.

"I don't know. It would be tough to sell," said the fence. "Does it come with directions?"

Hooks allowed as how he didn't know and the fence turned him down because that special television would be too easy to trace since apparently it was the only one of its kind.

This outraged Hooks Basumo. If it was only one of a kind it had to be worth more. He looked menacingly at the little man. He hinted about how little men could get hurt late at night. He noticed what a fire hazard the fence's home was.

"Hooks," said the fence, "I can get your bones broken for eighteen dollars. Get out of here."

Hooks raised a finger in obscene contempt and left muttering about the fence's lack of masculinity because if anyone ever gave Hooks the finger like that, they'd frigging get their frigging head handed to them.

At a newsstand, he waited for someone to drop a dollar for change, then snatched it and ran. You could get away with that if the owner really was blind. It was those sneaks who were only partially blind who could cross you up. They could see the outlines of hands moving.

But Hooks knew his newsstands. A man of respect was always careful. It was the punks who were careless. At a Dunkin Donut, he got a jelly filled and a cup of coffee light. He also picked up twenty-three cents in tips someone had carelessly left under a soggy napkin.

A black Cadillac Seville waited outside with

two men staring at Hooks. They had faces like pavements but with less warmth.

They had bulges in their silk suits. They did not smile.

When Hooks left the doughnut shop, the black car pulled up next to him on the curb.

"Hooks, get in," said the man next to the driver.

"I don't know you," said Hooks. The man in the front seat didn't say anything at all. He just stared at Hooks. Hooks got into the back seat.

They drove out of St. Louis proper on a route paralleling the Mississippi, fat with spring waters, wide as a lake. The car entered a fenced-off marina and Hooks saw a large white boat moored solid to a pier. The man in the front seat opened the rear door for Hooks.

"I didn't do it, I swear," said Hooks. And the man nodded him toward a gangplank.

At the top of the ramp, a round-faced man, sweating from the effort of keeping his fat supplied with blood and oxygen, nodded Hooks into a passageway.

"I didn't do it," said Hooks.

Hooks went down steps, his legs weak.

"I didn't do it," said Hooks to a man in a black tuxedo.

"I'm the butler," said the man.

When Hooks entered the room, and when he saw who sat on a large couch, he found himself unable to deny guilt. This was because the room spun around him and his legs were not beneath him and he was looking up. If he were looking up, he reasoned, his back must be on the floor. And who was giving him water?

Don Salvatore Massello himself. That's who was pressing a glass of water to his lips and asking if he were all right.

"Oh, Jesus," said Hooks. For now he was sure this was Massello. He had seen pictures in the newspapers and on television when Mr. Massello, surrounded by lawyers, had declined to talk to reporters.

There was the silver hair, the thin haughty nose, the immaculate dark eyebrows and the black eyes. And they were looking down at him and the lips were asking him if he were all right.

"Yes. Yes. Yes sir," said Hooks.

"Thank you for coming," said Mr. Massello.

"My pleasure and anytime, Mr. Massello, sir. An honor."

"And it is an honor to see you also, Mr. Basumo. May I call you Donald?" said Mr. Massello, helping Hooks to his feet and sitting him in a stuffed velvet chair and personally pouring him a glass of thick, sweet yellow Strega.

"Donald," said Mr. Massello, "we live in dangerous times."

"I didn't do it, sir. On my mother's sacred heart, I didn't do it."

"Do what, Donald?"

"Whatever, sir. I swear it."

Mr. Massello nodded with a tiredness that suggested the wisdom of the world.

"There are things men of respect must do to survive and I respect you for whatever you have done. I am proud to call you a friend, a brother."

Hooks offered to knock off any newsstand in the city for Mr. Massello, owned by a sighted person or not.

11

Don Salvatore Massello expressed gratitude for the most gracious offer but there was more important business at hand.

And he asked questions about the television set Donald had tried to sell to a fence. Had Donald seen it? Where was it? How did Donald hear of it? And getting an answer, Don Salvatore Massello asked about the girl, Janet Hawley, where she lived, where she worked and all manner of things concerning the girl.

"She don't mean shit to me, sir," said Hooks.

Mr. Massello understood that Donald was too serious a person to let his life be ruined by a skirt. Mr. Massello said this with a knowing smile. Mr. Massello led him to the door, assuring young Donald Basumo his future was secure. He would be a rich man.

And to show his good faith, he provided Donald with a room aboard the yacht that night. And two servants. They followed every instruction Hooks gave them, from bringing in booze and food and a young girl, except one request. Hooks wanted to take a walk in the fresh air. That they could not allow.

"You got everything you want right here. You're not leaving."

During the night, they awakened him and told him he could have his fresh air now. He didn't want it now. They told him he was taking it now.

It was 4:15 A.M. and quite dark. Hooks sat in the back seat of a car again and when they were well down the road headed toward St. Louis, he saw the marina lights come back on. He had left in darkness.

The car left the asphalt road and drove to the

yard of a small construction firm. Hooks was surprised to see Janet Hawley waiting for him. She wore a bright yellow print dress covered from the waist up with mud. She was resting. At the bottom of a ditch, with a very big dent in her head.

Hooks started to question the servants about this when one of them interrupted by banging a baseball bat into Donald (Hooks) Basumo's auditory cortex in his temporal lobe. It went crack. And made a very big and final dent in his skull.

Don Salvatore Massello was not around to hear the crack. He was on a plane bound for New York City where he would have something very important to report at the national meeting of the crime families.

Chapter Two

His name was Remo and he must have been cheating. James Merrick was praying for strength to complete his twentieth mile and the skinny bastard in blue had just passed him for the second time.

The next time would be three. Merrick's mind flitted back to the old sea adage of going down for the third time and he giggled hysterically. Suddenly his mirth turned bitter and he squeezed out, through clenched teeth:

"Hey, you. You, skinny. You, the guy in the tee shirt."

The man who had "Remo" written on his number card with a red magic marker turned his head back toward the huffing Merrick and pointed at himself.

"Who, me?" he said.

"Yeah. You. Remo. Wait up."

Remo slowed down and Merrick pulled his anguished legs, back and forth, back and forth, seemingly faster and faster. But he wasn't catching up; the distance between the two remained the same, no matter how hard he pushed his aching body.

"Come on. Slow down," yelled Merrick, in pain.

A moment later, Remo was no longer in front of him. He was directly beside Merrick, smiling distantly, running alongside him stride for stride.

"What do you want?" Remo said lightly.

Merrick stared at him, his eyes fogged with tears of exertion mingling with salty beads of sweat. The guy isn't even breathing hard, he thought.

"What's your number?" Merrick gasped.

Remo didn't answer. He just kept pace as they passed the Danvers town line.

Dammit, who was this maniac who wasn't even sweating? "You see this?" Merrick asked, jabbing the blue number six on his chest.

"Yeah," said Remo. "It's nice. That's called an Arabic number. Roman numbers are like they use for the Super Bowl. You know, x's and i's. Why do they call it an Arabic number? If Arabs could count real well, why don't their wars last more than a few days? Of course, maybe they'd rather lose fast than lose slow. I don't know."

The man was a loon, Merrick realized. "This is my number," Merrick puffed. "This means ... I'm the sixth ... person ... to sign up for ... this marathon. See? Now ... what's your number?"

Remo did not answer. Suddenly Merrick felt a light touch across his front and then a cool breeze ruffling his graying chest hair. He looked down

16

and saw a hole in his shirt where his number used to be clipped.

He looked back toward Remo but the man was gone. He had lengthened his stride and was pulling away from Merrick as if Merrick had been standing still. Remo's hands were busy at the front of his shirt and Merrick knew he was pinning on number six. James Merrick's number six.

This was all he needed. Four years of work and this bum was walking away with his race. And his number.

Merrick had wanted to run in the Boston Marathon ever since he was a youth. But four years before he had decided to plan for the Bicentennial Marathon. If he won that one, he would be remembered. For the better part of four years, he worked himself into condition. And then, starting in February, he really turned it on.

Every day after work, he would run the seven miles home, briefcase clutched to his well-tailored chest. He'd arrive to the barely concealed smirk of his wife, Carol, sweat soaking through his Arrow Pacesetter shirt and Brooks Brothers' suit.

Each evening, he practically had to scrape off his jockey shorts. He ruined his Florsheim cordovans the second night, but after that began carrying his Adidas track shoes to work in a paper bag.

Instead of lunch, he'd run in the men's room, stopping to wash or comb his hair every time someone came in. Coffee breaks were used for pushups in the utility room.

Soon his steamy figure became the subject of office chatter and "Merrick" jokes began to circulate.

When an anonymous caller told Merrick's wife

one night that there was an office pool betting on whether or not Merrick would die of a coronary before his pungent sweat smell claimed its first victim, she decided to have an intimate discussion with him.

"What the hell are you trying to prove?" she had said. "You're a Sunday athlete. The most running you should do is from the living room to the kitchen."

She liked the way that came out and laughed twice. James Merrick ignored her and kept running.

The Sunday before the race, Merrick had leaned over to his twelve-year-old son in front of the television set and said: "What do you think of your old dad winning the Marathon tomorrow, David?"

"Not now, Pop. Kojak is moving in. Who loves ya, baby?"

Merrick's head snapped up as if slapped to stare at the fat bald man on the Motorola television and he felt the bile rise. Kojak didn't have to run any marathon.

"I'm running twenty-six miles tomorrow, David." Merrick tried to smile but it was wasted on the back of his son's head. "Isn't that pretty good?"

"Yeah, Dad." Merrick felt some relief sweep over him.

"The Six Million Dollar Man did that tonight in an hour," David said.

Merrick saw the tide go out.

"Well, not really an hour, that was what they said it took him, but it was more like five minutes. In slow motion. Wow."

18

As his son ran around the room in slow motion, Merrick pictured himself on a cold beach and his eyes became as vacant as the horizon.

He'd show them. He'd show them all.

While Merrick had dressed the morning of the race, feeling everything was going to be perfect, Remo had awakened *knowing* things were perfect and it disgusted him.

It was wrong. It was wrong to sleep perfectly. To get up perfectly. To always be in perfect health. Misery, he decided, was the only thing that made life worth living.

Remo looked into his dark eyes in the bathroom mirror, then let them flick over his tanned face with its high cheekbones. His lean body, even with its extraordinarily thick wrists, gave no hint of the killing machine Remo had become.

Remo had watched himself shave. No wasted motion, easy smooth strokes.

Perfect.

Disgusting.

Why didn't he ever nick himself? Why didn't he get dragon mouth in the morning like everyone else?

Once upon a time he had. He remembered the cold stinging touch of the styptic pencil when he nicked his face shaving. But that had been years before, back in another life, when Remo Williams was just another patrolman in the Newark Police Department.

That was before he had been framed for a murder he didn't commit, and revived after a fake electrocution to work for a secret agency as its enforcer arm—code name Destroyer—in a war against crime.

That had been a long time ago and suddenly he did not want to look anymore at the plastic hotel room he had been staying in for three days. He did not want to speak to Chiun, the aged Korean assassin who was now motionless, asleep on a mat in the middle of the suite's living room floor.

It had been Chiun, the latest Master in centuries of masters from the small Korean village of Sinanju, who had changed Remo.

There had been ten years of prodding and probing, discipline, guidance, and technique and while Remo had long since stopped hating it all, he had never taken the time to determine if it was good.

He had climbed the mountain of his soul but forgotten to check whether he liked the view.

Remo stared at himself in the mirror. If he wanted right now, he could dilate or constrict the pupils of his eyes. He could raise the temperature of any part of his body six degrees. He could slow his heart beat to four a minute or speed it to 108 a minute, all without moving from this spot.

He wasn't even human anymore. He was just perfect.

Remo kicked open the bathroom door and walked quickly to the front door of the suite, past the frail-looking pile on the floor that was Chiun. Remo kicked open the front door too and since it was built to open inwards, most of the wood and plastic flew across the hall. The knob was later discovered by the manager, lodged in the soda machine three doors down.

A high squeaky voice stopped Remo halfway into the hall.

20

"You are troubled," Chiun said. "What is it?"

"I've just decided. I don't like being perfect."

Chiun laughed. "Perfect? Perfect? You? Heh, heh, heh. Do not waken me for any more jokes."

Remo gave Chiun's back a silent Bronx cheer, then went downstairs, through the red and brown tiled lobby of the hotel into the crisp April Boston morning.

Remo leaned against the outside front door of the hotel and started searching himself.

"Pardon me, sir," said a bellboy.

"Don't bother me," Remo said. "Can't you see I'm perfect?"

"But, sir . . ."

"One more word and you'll be blowing your nose from the back."

The bellboy left. Remo thought of the first time he had met Chiun. The old Oriental was shuffling toward him in a gymnasium at Folcroft Sanitarium in Rye, New York, the secret headquarters of the secret organization CURE. Chiun had at first looked like a skinny skeleton covered with yellow parchment . . .

"Pardon me, sir," said the bell captain, who didn't particularly want anyone's pardon. He had been laying his bet on No Preservatives Added in the fifth at Suffolk Downs when the bellboy had made him aware of the man standing outside.

"Pardon me, sir," the bell captain repeated, "but what are you doing?"

"What does it look like I'm doing?" Remo asked.

The bell captain thought carefully. You never knew what might show up when you had a hotel this close to Huntington Avenue, Boston's answer to Dante's Eighth Circle.

"It looks, sir, like you're leaning against a building with just a towel on."

Remo looked down. The bell captain was right.

"So?" said Remo.

"Well." The bell captain paused. "It's our towel."

"I'm a paying customer," Remo said.

"Do you have a key, sir?"

"I left it in my other towel," Remo said.

"How are you going to get back into your room then?"

"Don't worry. I'll manage," Remo said.

"Aren't you a little bit cold?"

"I'm too perfect to be cold," Remo said and turned away from the man who was making it difficult for him to think.

The bell captain shrugged and went back to his station. He would give the wierdo five minutes before calling the hotel detective. In the meantime, he called his bookie to put in his bet on No Preservatives Added who later broke her foreleg coming around the first turn. The bell captain's bet at the Wonderland dog races in Revere leaped at the automatic rabbit and got electrocuted. The Red Sox lost 17 to 1. The bell captain's oldest son was booked for possession, his wife got another day deeper into the change of life, and his dog got hit by a car. Looking back on it the next day, he would bet that his run of bad luck began with the warm-blooded guy leaning against the hotel wall with just a towel on.

Remo was still thinking, trying to remember just when it was that he had become perfect.

He had met Chiun in the gymnasium, and he

22

had had a gun in his hand and was ordered to kill the old Oriental for a night off from training. For a night off, he would have done anything, and he had fired six shots point blank at Chiun and all of them had missed. He certainly hadn't been perfect that night.

"Pardon me, sir," said a greasy young girl.

"Don't bother me," Remo said.

"Oh, it won't be a bother, sir," the girl said. "Would you like to take a personality test?"

Remo looked at the girl. She was wearing a pasteboard tag that said, "Hello, my name is Margie from the School of Powerology." Her hair hung down across her shiny pock-marked face like spaghetti in clam sauce. Through dirty oil-streaked glasses, her eyes were a dull powdery brown.

"Sure," said Remo. "I'm trying to find out why I'm perfect."

"We can help you to know yourself better, that will be fifty cents, please."

"Pardon?" Remo said.

"You *are* taking the test?"

"Yes."

"Well, it's fifty cents for my time and the cost of the test paper, sir."

"Can I owe it to you?"

"Don't you have it on you?"

"Not so you'd notice," Remo said.

Margie stared him up and down, then licked her lips. "I guess you could give it to me later," she said. She giggled and blushed, and the sudden flush of color combined with her natural pallor to make her look purple.

"What is your name, sir?"

"Kay Kyser from the College of Musical Knowledge."

"Very good," Margie said, pulling open a loose-leaf folder she had been holding. "Question number one. Are you happy?"

"No," said Remo.

"Then, sir, you should get our booklet: *A Happier You Through Powerology,* which is only $3.98 for the first copy and $2.50 for each one afterwards."

"I will seriously consider it," Remo said. "Do you have another question."

"Yes, sir. Lots of questions," she said staring at his chest again. "Question number two. Do you lay, I mean, like your friends?"

"What friends?" Remo asked.

"Yes or no," Margie said. "It has to be yes or no, I can't fit 'what friends' into the space."

"Can't you write smaller?"

"It'll come out 'wha fri.' "

"Okay," Remo said. "No."

"Oh. Then a must for your library would be the *Powerology Guide for Better Friendships or How to Win People to Your Side through Powerology.* Right now, you could have it for only $2.95, for a limited time, of course."

"I'll keep it in mind."

Margie was staring at his belly button. "Of course, something could be arranged," she said.

"Question three," Remo said.

"Oh, yes," she said, shaking her head and sending beads of greasy dirt flying. "How do you rape, I mean, rate your love life on a scale of one to ten?"

"None," said Remo. "Minus six. Minus ninety."

24

"Oh, that's a shame, but nothing that couldn't be remedied by *How to Pick up Girls and Score Through Powerology* for only $4.95 or letting me come up to your room."

"You're losing your scientific dispassion," Remo said.

"Don't tell me that. I can see rape in your eyes."

"That's because your glasses are dirty," Remo said.

"Look, fella, I'll knock up ... I mean, off the fifty-cent service charge."

"Not now."

"This is my last offer. I knock off the service charge, throw in a Powerology book of massage and pay for dinner afterwards. What more could you want?"

"Your sudden and complete disappearance," Remo said.

"Too bad. I could have helped you find yourself," Margie said.

Remo felt sorry for her because she wasn't perfect like him. He set the time as 10:27. Chiun's daily ration of soap operas would begin at noon sharp.

"Look," Remo said. "Come back in two hours and go up to Suite 1014. You'll recognize it 'cause it doesn't have a door. Just go in and make yourself at home until I get back." He turned her around and patted her behind. "Run along now. Remember. About two hours. Bring your friends. Bring all your friends."

Margie giggled and took off toward Kenmore Square like a rocket.

Remo wandered down across the Christian

Science Center and toward the Prudential Building, the second tallest skyscraper in Boston. It used to be the first until another insurance company had built a solid glass monstrosity designed to reflect the sky and hundreds of birds killed themselves every day by flying into it.

Hundreds of people were milling about in the Prudential Mall. Remo really did not notice them because he was watching his legs move almost perfectly. He was so intent on his feet he almost walked into a middle-aged man bouncing up and down.

"Hey. Watch what you're doing," the man said.

Remo looked up and saw the crowd milling around him, then looked back to the graying man in his white shorts with red racing stripes, gray sweat shirt, and Adidas sneakers.

"What are you doing?" asked Remo.

"Getting set," the man said.

"For what?"

"For what? Are you kidding? Where have you been, man?"

"Well, I was in Korea for a while."

"Oh, yeah. I was in Korea too," the man said. "What were you doing?"

"Wiping out most of the standing army," said Remo, looking out over all the bobbing heads. "What is all this?"

"It's the Boston Marathon," said the man who had been to Korea himself for awhile. "We run to Brickton, Massachusetts, and back."

"What for?"

The graying man looked at Remo as if he were crazy. The towel probably helped, although, among all the shorts, it looked just like an eccentric kilt.

"How far is Brickton?" asked Remo.

"Thirteen miles," the man said.

"I'll be right back," Remo said. Fifteen minutes later, Remo stepped out of a men's shop dressed like the man he had been speaking to—in white shorts with red stripes, a gray sweatshirt, and Adidas running shoes, all charged to his hotel room and verified by the store clerk with a call to the hotel which informed the clerk frostily that the gentleman from Room 1014 had infinite credit, whether he was wearing a towel or not.

Remo joined all the runners in the sun of downtown Boston as they gathered around the entrance to the Prudential Building from Boylston Avenue.

A heavy, red-haired man was waving the starting gun and shouting, "Five minutes. Five minutes."

Suddenly, hundreds of people started leaping, breathing deep, stretching, and running in place all around Remo. He felt like laughing. Warm-up exercises were a joke.

Early on in his training, Chiun had told him: "One must always be ready. We do not practice eating before meals. Why practice running before running?"

"Hey," came a voice from behind Remo, who turned into the already perspiring face of the gray-haired man he had met before.

"Going to race, huh? That's great. Just great. My name's Merrick, by the way. James Merrick. No offense or anything, but no one's going to beat me today. Hey, you better get a number. See you at the finish. If you finish."

The best Remo could do was to find a red magic marker and to scrawl "REMO" on the back of a parking ticket he lifted from a windshield. And then the gun sounded and Remo was off like a speeding bullet. James Merrick saw him pulling away and smiled to himself. Marathons were filled with people like that—people with no serious thought of completing the race, who broke like sprinters, ran a mile as fast as they could, then dropped out and spent the rest of their lives bragging about how they had led the Boston Marathon for awhile.

That had been at the race's start, but now Remo had passed Merrick for the second time, twenty miles later, and to add insult to injury he had just stolen Merrick's big number six.

Merrick tried to cling mentally to the slim thick-wristed figure but Remo soon disappeared over a hill.

Merrick plugged on, no longer sure whether he was winning or losing the race, his mind growing as fatigued as his body, and as he crossed the Charlestown line, he saw Remo again, this time passing him with a bright blue six on his shirt.

Merrick tried to scream, come back with my number, you frigging maniac who isn't even sweating, running circles around me with your frigging red Remo. But the exertion would have been too much.

Crossing into Danvers, he started to cry tears of frustration when the broadly-smiling Remo passed him for the fourth time. James Merrick wanted to beg, please, please, crazy person, don't you know how much this means to me? Win the race if you want to, but leave me alone. Please?

Finally Merrick crossed into Boston. He felt renewed. Only two hours had passed. He had pushed himself and his time was better than had ever been seen in the Boston Marathon. This he knew. He swept forward with new vitality. His second wind had arrived.

And left as Remo passed him for the fifth time a second later.

James Merrick collapsed with an anguished gasp. He later didn't remember how long he huddled, head in his arms on the side of the road into Boston with his dirty sneakers and ripped sweat shirt, but when he looked up it seemed darker. He didn't see people pass him. He didn't care. Instead he stumbled to a bus stop, caught a bus, and got off three blocks from home.

What would he say? Should he stay in a hotel? No, he hadn't any wallet with him. What the hell. Probably no one had even noticed he was gone. Carol had still been asleep when Merrick left that morning and David had been watching Speed Racer and hadn't even turned when his father said "So long."

James Merrick slowly plodded up the steps, fighting tears. It wasn't his loss of the race that got him: it was his own failure. He walked into the house.

"Jim, is that you?"

"Yes," he croaked.

"What are you doing here?" his wife cried, running down from upstairs, "Everybody's been looking for you. I've been getting calls since two o'clock."

"I don't want any calls," Merrick said miserably.

Carol's face became stern. "Now I know you're tired but you go right back to Copley Square and accept your trophy."

Merrick managed "Wha?"

"They've been looking all over for you. Nobody ever ran that fast. Like a sprinter they said. Going so fast all they could see was your number six." She looked down at his sweatshirt.

"Oh, you poor thing. It must have gotten ripped off. You go up and lie down. I'll call the athletic committee and tell them you're here."

"Where's David?" Merrick asked.

"Out telling all his friends that you won. Now, go lie down, will you?"

Merrick heard and obeyed. He didn't care how long his nirvana lasted. If it only lasted a moment, it was still one moment of perfection, more than most men had.

A moment before he reached his personal cloud nine, he thanked all his lucky stars for a gray-dressed, non-perspiring figment of his imagination named Remo.

At that moment, Remo was rejecting an assignment and, because he was perfect, trying to do it in a nice way.

"Blow it out your ears," Remo said on the telephone to Dr. Harold W. Smith, head of CURE. "I don't care how many Mafia thugs are meeting in New York. You do something about them."

"Remo," Smith said, "I'm not asking you to do anything. I'm alerting you to stay ready in case something comes up on short notice. There hasn't been a meeting like this since Appalachia."

"Well, I don't like to deal with the Mafia anymore," Remo said.

"Why not, pray tell?" Smith asked, his voice even over the telephone a citric acid bath.

"Because I'm perfect and I don't like to dirty my hands on the unworthy."

And for the second time that day, someone laughed at Remo's claim to perfection.

"Funny, huh?" Remo said. "If that gives you a laugh, watch the TV news tonight about the Boston Marathon. I ran the course five times and still won. Let's see one of your dipwiddle computers do that."

"I'll call you when an assignment presents itself," Smith said in a resigned voice.

"Whatever makes you happy," Remo said breezily.

"I liked you better when you were imperfect," Smith said, but Remo did not hear him. He had already hung up and, still wearing his track clothes, trotted away from the street corner telephone booth and headed back toward his hotel.

Chapter Three

Don Salvatore Massello was angry and disgusted with himself.

He sat in the back of his chauffeured limousine as it picked its way through Manhattan's late afternoon traffic, and hid himself behind clouds of cigar smoke and reflected that organized crime looked organized only because everything else in the country was so disorganized. How could one attach the label of "organized" to what had gone on this afternoon?

Massello had been sure of himself as he sat with the twenty-seven other leaders on the Mafia's ruling council in the string of suites in the Hotel Pierre, overlooking New York's Central Park.

And when it had come his turn, he had reported glowingly on the progress the organization was making in the Midwest, and then had turned his attention to the marvelous television invention he had learned about.

What he wanted, he explained, was authorization to spend "any amount of money" to obtain the machine and its inventor.

He had expected routine and immediate approval and was startled when Pietro Scubisci of the New York families, a seventy-five-year-old man with a rumpled collar and a grease-stained suit said, "What amount is any amount, Don Salvatore?"

Massello had shrugged, as if the amount was the least important of things. "Who knows?" he said. "I know it is important that we have the inventor with us, so that we and we alone control this new device. Any amount is a cheap amount, Don Pietro."

"I do not like people who spend their time watching television," Scubisci said. "Too many today, too much time looking at pictures."

The other men around the table had nodded, and Don Salvatore Massello had realized his proposal was in trouble and that he had made a mistake bringing it here to ask approval. He should just have gone ahead and bought the invention himself.

"You know who likes television?" said Fiavorante Pubescio of the Los Angeles family. "Your Arthur Grassione likes television."

"Arthur is a nice boy," said Scubisci with finality.

"He watches television," said Pubescio gingerly.

"Yes, but he is a nice boy," said Scubisci, defending his nephew. "Don Salvatore," he said, "you go ahead for us and try to buy that television picture machine. But any amount is too much. Five hundred thousand is enough for a college professor. And when you go there, take Arthur Grassione with you. He knows all about television." Scubisci looked at Pubescio. "Arthur watches television so he will know what people are saying about us," he said triumphantly.

"I know, Don Pietro," said Pubescio.

"And if your professor will not sell you his television set, well, then Arthur will take it from him," Scubisci told Don Salvatore Massello. The old man looked around the table. "Agreed?" he asked.

No one spoke, but twenty-six heads nodded toward him.

"Done," said Scubisci. "Who is next?"

And that had been that and now Don Salvatore Massello was headed downtown to meet a man he had met many years before and had detested immediately: Arthur Grassione, the chief enforcer for the national organization.

Felix the Cat had been the first. Mickey Mouse was originally supposed to be but there had been some last-minute problems with the Disney studios and the cat was brought in.

So, if not for some minor trouble in an office in Southern California, Mickey Mouse would not only have had his face plastered across a garden, decorated millions of wrist watches and made it with Minnie Mouse on dirty posters, but he would have been the first thing seen on national television for eight and one-half minutes at the New York Worlds' Fair in 1939.

Instead, it was Felix and at that time Felix had been a miracle.

All the people there had oohed and aahed and said "amazing" and "wonderful" and then forgot all about it. But 19-year-old Arthur Grassione had seen and understood and never forgot. And since then he had watched many other miracles.

At thirty, Arthur, a rising soldato in the New York crime families, watched Uncle Miltie in drag. At thirty-eight, Grassione, rising Mafia star, watched Your Show of Shows. At forty-one, he watched the live, unrehearsed murder of a Presidential assassin, and at forty-six, he watched the Vietnam war in thirty-minute slots with several sixty-minute segments. At fifty, he was the mob's number-one enforcer in the country and he watched men walk on the moon.

Television had been Arthur Grassione's major educational experience and through it he had learned that blacks were co-stars, Italians made great heroes, fat men were always funny, and Chinese were spies, servants, or gardeners except for Charlie Chan who was really Hawaiian.

And now the fifty-five-year-old Arthur Grassione was watching another miracle and he was not happy. He was watching the closing of another of Uncle Pietro's numbers rackets.

Grassione sat with his back to Vince Marino, his number-one flunky, and stared at the big Sony set as a sickly green announcer told of the major gambling bust by the Manhattan district attorney's office.

Grassione spun in his chair and stared at Marino, then pounded his fists on his huge oaken desk.

"You know that 154 chinks worked two hours each to make all the works in that frigging thing so I could see our own boys get arrested in living green and white?"

Marino noticed that the color contrast was moved all the way over to green. He got up and moved toward the set.

"The color dial, boss. It's a little off. I'll get it."

Grassione screamed at him. "Hands off. There's nothing wrong with the frigging set. The gooks made it that way. The gooks can't make anything right. Sit down."

During his tirade, a small bit of saliva had spiraled out of Grassione's mouth onto his left lapel. Grassione desperately tore at his jacket as if it were trying to eat him. He ripped it off and hurled it across the room.

As Marino slid back into his straight-backed chair, Grassione yelled, "Grease ball! Grease ball! Where the hell are you? Get in here!"

A door on the left hand side of the office opened slowly and a short, thin, pop-eyed Oriental shuffled in and stood still before Grassione, his eyes buried in the floor.

"Grease ball," Grassione cried again. His voice had the happy intensity of a Doberman pinscher chancing upon an injured bird. "About time you're here. Get my jacket and clean it."

The small Oriental began to turn toward the jacket heaped on the floor.

"And not . . ." Grassione began.

The Oriental turned.

"And not at your goddam Chink laundry either. Get it to an Italian Laundry. There you'll see clean. But you don't know what clean is, do you, you yellow slob?"

Vince Marino fidgeted in his chair as he always did when Grassione was abusing Edward Leung. The chair creaked and Grassione shot Marino a vicious look while Leung began to shuffle toward the jacket on the floor.

Grassione's eyes moved back to the moving Chinese.

"Slower, you stupid coolie," he screamed.

Edward Leung slowed down and carefully slid his left foot in front of his right, rocked, slid his right food forward, rocked, left, rock, right, rock, left...

"That's better," Grassione said.

Leung reached the jacket and leaned forward, almond eyes narrowing, his hand opening slowly, as if waiting for something to happen.

Marino looked away. He didn't like Chinese any more than the next guy—unless the next guy happened to be Chinese—but this disgusted him.

Grassione stood still, mouth open in anticipation, until Leung's hand was an inch from the jacket on the floor.

"Your gloves," he yelled. "Where are your gloves? You ain't getting my clothes full of your yellow germs."

Edward Leung closed his eyes and sighed inwardly as he reached to his back pocket for his thick gardener's gloves. He had never worked in a garden, not even when he was growing up in Columbus, Ohio, but Grassione wanted to believe that all Chinese worked in gardens so Leung carried gardener's gloves.

38

He picked up the jacket gingerly between right thumb and index finger.

"Now you get that cleaned," Grassione said. "And hurry it up. I've got an important guest coming and I don't have no jacket and it's your fault, you dumb, stupid, frigging yellow gook chink."

Grassione stared at Edward Leung until the door closed behind the small yellow man. Then Grassione moved to a closet behind his desk. Slamming it open, he pulled a perfectly cleaned and pressed jacket from a bright wooden hanger.

As Grassione slid on the dark silk jacket, a perfect match to his trousers, Marino looked back at the Sony where two people were talking happily in their sunny playroom about how wonderful it was not only to get their clothes soft but to keep the colors bright as well. The black man was just asking his TV wife, in soothingly pleasant tones, how she got his shirts so white when Grassione's hand shot up to smack the set off. As the green dot in the middle of the screen began to fade, Grassione whirled back to Marino.

He leaned forward over the oak desk and said with a smile: "What do you think, Vince? What's Massello going to want?"

Vince Marino desperately searched the thick pile rug for the right words. "I don't know, Chief. I guess he wants us to hit somebody."

He looked up and saw Grassione rise to his full five-feet-nine, and walk tightly around to the front of the desk. He stopped in front of Marino, smiling inwardly as he approvingly gauged his effect on his lieutenant.

"Yeah," Grassione said. "But not just anybody.

Massello got his own people in St. Louis that can do hitting."

Marino shrugged. "Who then?"

"Massello's pretty smart," Grassione said. "Smart enough that some people figure someday he's going to be capo of capos. The way I figure it is he's got a special hit for us."

"Special?" said Marino, realizing at that moment that his boss with his shiny suit, his grease-slicked hair, and his oily skin looked like a plaster doll that had been deep-fried.

"Yeah. Special. Like maybe that guy who's been messing us up around the country. The one who got Johnny Deuce and Verillio and Salvatore Polastro. The guy who's been devastating us."

He pronounced the word as *dee*-vastating, but Marino did not correct him because Grassione had once told him he had spent "a lot of bucks learning to talk good." So he nodded.

But later when Marino had left the room, and Don Salvatore Massello had arrived, Grassione was disappointed to find out that the hit was only a maybe-hit, if the man wouldn't deal, and the man was only a college professor. He stayed depressed until Massello explained to him that the man had invented a new kind of television machine which Grassione took as an insult because he liked television just the way it was.

"Sure, we'll hit him, Don Salvatore," he said.

Massello smiled and shook his head. "No. We will hit him only if he will not deal with us. Those are Don Pietro's instructions."

"Whatever he wants," Grassione said. "Whatever you want, Don Salvatore."

"Good," Massello said. He made arrangements

40

to meet Grassione later, then hurriedly left the lower Broadway office. He felt in desperate need of a shower.

After Massello had left, Grassione turned on the television set, just in time to catch an independent station's sports report. But it was showing a film clip of some stupid guy winning some stupid race in Boston and because Grassione was not interested in sports on which he could not bet, he turned from the set and pressed a buzzer.

A moment later, Edward Leung entered his office. He paused inside the door of the darkened office, his almond eyes looking first at Grassione, then at the green-imaged television set.

"Tell me, wise one, what do you see?" Grassione asked.

"I see nothing," Leung said.

Grassione half-rose in his chair. "Hey, I don't pay you for 'I don't see nothing's.' "

"That is what I see."

"Get outta here, you Chink bastard."

Leung shrugged and opened the door behind him. He turned one more time to look at Grassione, then at the television screen which showed the winner of the Boston Marathon, racing past the finish line so fast he was only a blur on camera.

"All of life ends in death and dreams," Leung said.

"Get outta here. Go pack your rickshaw, coolie. We're going to St. Louis."

Chapter Four

Fourteen people fell in love with Remo as he returned to the hotel.

Several women on the outskirts of the marathon crowd where it thinned out two blocks from the finish line tried jogging alongside him, gasping as they tried to give him their telephone numbers. He got rid of them by telling them mincingly, "My woommate Bart would never appwove."

One woman passenger in a car saw Remo and grabbed her boyfriend so hard he almost drove into the entrance of the Todd Private High School. A cashier and a candy girl in a theater, along with an usher whose sexual preferences were somewhat unclear, followed him with their eyes.

So did a black airlines reservation clerk who decided she would grow her hair back long and uncurl it from its Afro. She'd move from Dorchester and walk no more in South Boston. She'd gain a little weight and stop being such a tease. She'd meet him one night in the reading room of the library and from that night on be his slave, cook, cleaner, maid, fox, and mammy. Screw the movement. Screw women's lib. His. Now, then, and forever.

There were more, and Remo was aware of them, sensing the slight pressure of stares on him, but he couldn't be bothered now. After all, sex was just another technique—squeeze here for a purr, touch there for a gasp—and he had more important things on his mind than techniques. His techniques were perfect; everything he did was perfect. So why wasn't he happy? Didn't perfection include happiness?

Remo slowed down as he passed an around-the-clock bookstore, and jogged inside.

The clerk at the front check-out counter looked at Remo and said: "The exercise books are in the back on the right. Jogging on the top shelf."

"Where's your dictionaries?" Remo asked.

The clerk had a beard that grew up his cheeks, almost to his eye sockets. Now the beard flickered as he winked to the clerk next to him, trying to gift-wrap a copy of *The Prophet*. "What are you looking up? Jockstrap?" the clerk said.

"Actually, no," Remo said. "I was thinking of surly, insolent, asshole, and fatality." He did not wink.

"Over there," the clerk said, pointing a trembling index finger at a low, flat counter.

Remo found the thickest dictionary and skimmed through it:

"Per-fek' - shen: 1) the quality or state of being perfect, as a) freedom from fault or defect."

He looked through all the definitions, but none of them mentioned happiness. He was disappointed.

On his way out, the clerk asked Remo: "Find what you wanted?"

"Yeah. Did you know I can be perfect without being happy?"

Before the clerk could answer, Remo was back on the street. He did not feel like going straight back to his hotel room, so he decided to carry his perfection caravan into the Roxbury ghetto of Boston.

The sight of a white man, running down the street after dark, in track shorts, caused much hilarity in Roxbury, but it stopped when nobody could catch him, not even Freddy (Panther) Davis, who last year had set the inner-city record for the fastest 440 ever run in stolen Keds.

The April night was chilling as Remo headed back toward his bright hotel. He looked up toward their room where he imagined Chiun sat at peace and decided he did not want to go up, not yet. So he jogged along Boylston Street until it intersected with Massachusetts Avenue, the sidewalks bathed by the eerie eyes of the passing cars on both the city streets and the Massachusetts Turnpike which passed under that point.

Remo stepped up to the guard rail over the turnpike and stared out at the impassive automobiles of the anything-but-impassive men and women who were born, became neurotic, argued, fought, questioned, reasoned, loved, screwed, killed, sought immortality, then died.

He thought about each one moving toward him and wondering where they were coming from and what they had done. He saw the cars on the other side disappear around a distant bend and wondered where their drivers were going and what they might do.

And then he had it. It was all clear, why he could be unhappy even though perfect.

Suddenly Remo knew where he was going and where all those cars were going.

Remo was going to a hotel.

Everybody else in the world was going home.

And Remo would never go home. Home was a wife, kids. But it would only be a matter of time before a wife would tap him on the back when he wasn't looking and she would wind up with many important internal organs atomized. And kids? By the time his were of school age, they probably would have wiped out half the block, which might be hard to explain to the P.T.A. "You see, friends and neighbors, the children's father is the world's most perfect killing machine and they're just chips off the old block, heh, heh."

But there was no reason he couldn't have a home. A house. A place other than a hotel room. He could do without kids anyway. Bringing them up nowadays was risky, 'cause if they didn't turn out to be junkies, they stood a good chance of turning out to be freakos like that obnoxious Margie from the School of . . .

"Oh, balls," Remo said aloud.

As he tore off toward his hotel, an old lady clapped her hands over the ears of the twelve-year-old boy walking with her and shouted after

46

him: "What the fuck's wrong with you? Can't you see I got a child with me, for Christ's sake?"

Remo hit the hotel steps three at a time, he took six at a time on the second and third floors and made the last seven flights in seven bounds.

He burst onto his floor, ruining his second door of the day, and jumped to the open entrance to his room.

Chiun sat in the middle of the floor, facing the door, his eyes closed, his mouth creased in a small smile. In the four corners of the room were four girls, their thumbs in their mouths, their rears pointed skyward.

Chiun opened his eyes as Remo entered and looked around.

"Oh, it is the perfect one," Chiun said, and then cackled. "Heh, heh, heh. All hail the perfect one."

"All right, knock it off," Remo said. "What'd you do to them?"

"Nothing but what they asked for," Chiun said. "Barging in here through a door that the perfect one had destroyed, a perfectly good door, and demanding to see wonderful Remo, and all the while, I am sitting here, minding my business, taking a few moments of pleasure from *All My Offspring* while you are out, gallivanting around ... where were you while all this was going on?"

Remo refused to be sidetracked. "What'd you do to them?" he said, but before Chiun could answer, one of the girls moaned.

Remo walked over to the sound. Looking closer, he realized the girl was not only alive, but smiling broadly. So were the other three, including Margie who held a copy of *The Powerology Guide to Sexual Fulfillment* in her dirty fist.

"Take them out of here," Chiun said. "In a perfect manner, of course. Heh, heh, heh. Just as I always thought. You are perfect for taking out garbage."

Remo, relieved to find that the four bodies weren't just bodies, did not even argue. He reached down to the hulk of Margie and grabbed her under the stomach. She arched slowly, muttered "Fantastic," then wrapped her body around Remo's hand, like a kitten if a kitten could be called sex-crazed. Remo lifted her like the handle of a Samsonite two-suiter and deposited her on her feet outside the suite. She seemed to float down the hall toward the elevator. Remo shot a leering look at Chiun.

"Dirty old man," he said.

"They are reliving their childhoods," Chiun said, "which all happen to be pleasant ones. Wipe that disgusting look off your lecherous muffin face. The Master of Sinanju is above such things."

He turned his back and looked out the window as Remo deposited the other three girls in the hall and pushed them off, like walking dolls sold by sidewalk peddlers, in the direction of the elevators.

When Remo went back in the room, he brought with him the remnants of the door, which he propped in place.

"No one came to fix this door?" he asked.

"They did. But I told them to come back when the Perfect One was here. Heh, heh, heh."

"What did you do to those girls?" Remo asked.

"They interrupted me. I put them to sleep and

48

made them feel good. But what did you do to-day?"

"I made a decision. I want a house," Remo said.

"Good," said Chiun. "So do I. I will take the one in electrical Washington."

"What?" Remo said.

"It was you who explained it to me. About electricity, the different currents. Electrical Washington."

"Washington, D.C., doesn't have anything to do with electricity," Remo said. "D.C. doesn't stand for direct current."

"You told me it did," Chiun said petulantly.

"Well, it does sometimes. But not this time."

"I am glad you are perfect," Chiun said, "because you will always be able to tell me when it means direct current and when it doesn't. But I still want that big white house there."

"The President lives there," Remo said.

"How long will it take him to move?" Chiun asked.

"He's not moving."

"The President would deny us this?" Chiun asked.

"I deny us this," Remo said.

"I will never forget this, Remo. First you lie to me about electricity and then you will not let me have a house which is little enough to ask, considering all I have done for you," Chiun said.

"Why that house, Chiun?" asked Remo who felt himself sinking into an endless pit of explanation and counter-explanation. "Why is that house so important to you?"

"I don't care about the house," Chiun said. "It

is what one can do there. I have seen this maker of automobiles . . ."

"Ah, geez, Chiun."

"You go back on that explanation, too?"

Remo remained silent.

"I have seen this automobile maker beckon merely and I have seen Barbra Streisand come to this big ugly white house in electrical Washington. This I have seen. And I, I could stand in the glorious palaces of noble Sinanju and beckon until my fingers turn to dust and Barbra Streisand would not come."

"So, we're back to Barbra Streisand."

"Yes," said Chiun.

"Well, let's forget Barbra Streisand and let's forget the White House. I just want a plain house. To live in."

"It must be a perfect house," Chiun said. "To match you. Would a beauty wrap herself in rags?"

"All right. Enough," Remo said. "I've been graumed all day and now I've figured out what it is. I want to be like other people."

Chiun shook his head in sad bewilderment. "I have heard of the cat who would be king. But I never heard of a king who would be a cat. I have given you Sinanju, and now you want to be like other people? Like you were? Eating meat, sleeping the day away, groveling and miserable? This is what you want?"

"No, Chiun. I just want a house. Like yours in Sinanju," Remo lied, because he regarded Chiun's home in Sinanju as the ugliest thing ever built in the world.

"I understand," Chiun said. "It is good to have a beautiful house."

Remo nodded. He felt warmed and comforted by Chiun's understanding of his feelings.

"And someday we can invite Barbra Streisand to visit," Chiun said brightly.

"Right, right, right, right, right," said Remo in exasperation.

"Don't forget it," Chiun said. "Five rights do not allow a wrong. Heh, heh, heh."

The telephone rang an hour later, after Remo and Chiun had dined on rice and fish and Chiun had "done the dishes" by sailing the plates out the open window into the Boston night, where they produced seventeen unconfirmed U.F.O. sightings, and the formation of a new committee, the Boston League for Astronomical Truth whose first act was to print stationery so they could mail a fund-raising letter.

The caller was Smith.

"Hello, Doctor Smith," Remo said politely. "I'm so glad you called."

"Remo," Smith began, then checked himself. "Wait a minute," he said. " 'Doctor Smith?' "

"That's right. The good, wise Doctor Smith," Remo said.

"Remo, what do you want?"

"No, sir, you first. After all, you called and you are my superior . . ."

"Everyone is," Chiun snickered.

" . . . you are my superior and I'd like to hear what's on your mind."

"Yes, well, remember I told you about the Mafia meeting in New York?"

"Of course, sir," Remo replied. He looked out at

51

the sky and wondered why birds did not fly at night. Sure, they were busy going places in the daytime but didn't they ever have errands to run at night?

"Well, we've just learned that Arthur Grassione, the head Mafia hit man, and Salvatore Massello, the St. Louis head man, are on their way to Edgewood University outside St. Louis."

"Perhaps, sir," Remo said, "they've decided to mend their ways, to enroll as students, and live a new life." Remo counted seven sets of wing lights in the night-time sky. The sky was getting as crowded as the earth. Maybe birds only flew on off-hours.

"No, I don't think that's it," said Smith. "It cost us a man but we've learned they're on their way to try to get some kind of new television invention. There's a professor there named William Wooley or Wooley Westhead or something like that."

Terrific, Remo thought. I want a house and Smith wants to talk about Wooley-headed college professors. He said, "I understand."

"Massello is a new kind of Mafia don," Smith said. "He's bright and subtle and chances are he's going to be the next national boss. Now if you can do something to stop him . . ."

"Certainly," Remo said. "Are you done, sir? Is that all?"

"Yes," Smith said warily.

"I want a frigging house," Remo yelled. "I'm tired of living in these frigging hotels. I want a house. If you don't give me a house, I'm quitting. Well?"

"If I give you a house will you promise always to be polite?" Smith asked.

"No."

"Will you promise to always carry out missions faithfully and without questioning my orders?"

"Of course not. Most of the time your orders are so stupid they're painful."

"If I give you a house, do you promise to take care of Massello and Grassione? *And* find out what they're after?"

"I might," Remo said.

"Do it first and then we'll talk about the house," Smith said.

"Will we talk about it yes or will we talk about it no?" Remo asked.

"We'll talk about it maybe," Smith said.

"Then maybe I'll take care of Grassello and Massione," Remo said.

"Massello and Grassione," Smith said. "Come on, Remo, this is important."

"So's my house," said Remo.

Chiun hissed, "Ask him to increase the tribute to my village." Remo waved him off.

"Smitty," he said. "We'll meet you in St. Louis and discuss this some more."

"I can't get away," Smith protested.

"You have to get away. This all won't wait. If you don't go to St. Louis," he said, "don't look for us there."

Smith paused for a moment, to try to unravel the logic of that sentence, then surrendered to it. "I'll be there tomorrow," he said.

"Good," said Remo. "Bring enough money for a house."

He hung up and told Chiun, "We're going to St. Louis."

"Good," said Chiun. "Let us go now."

"Why the hurry?"

"Soon those four cowlike females will come to their senses and they will be back. What do I need with four servants?"

Remo nodded.

"When I have you," Chiun said.

Chapter Five

Dr. Harold W. Smith woke up at 3:45 A.M. He let his wife sleep as he went into the kitchen and prepared one slice of whole wheat toast, light, without butter, one two-and-a-half-minute egg and a four-ounce glass filled with two ounces of lemon juice and two ounces of prune juice, his only concession to the possibility of originality in the kitchen.

He followed the breakfast with a glass of lukewarm water, then reentered the bedroom where he picked up the two-suiter he had packed the night before, planted a kiss on the cheek of his still-sleeping wife, who tried to swat it away, and then drove to his office.

Something had been niggling at his mind since he had first gotten the name from an informant of Professor William Westhead Wooley of Edgewood University, and he planned to make one last check.

He was waved through the gate of Folcroft Sanitarium, which served as headquarters for CURE, the secret organization he had headed since its formation. When he parked his car in his private parking space in the otherwise empty lot, he took a notebook from his pocket and jotted down a reminder to do something about the front gate security which was becoming a little bit too lax, even for an institution masquerading as a sanitarium for the wealthy ill and an educational research center.

Alone in his office, Smith quickly composed a retrieval memo to be fed into CURE's computers. He wanted anything on Wooley, Edgewood University, and television inventions.

The computer returned only a trade journal report that said "word has it that a major breakthrough in television technology has almost been perfected and an announcement is expected soon."

That was all.

Smith crumpled up the report and dropped it into the shredder basket next to his desk. He set a series of locks that would prevent anyone but himself from tapping into the CURE computer system for information, then turned out the lights, locked up behind him, and went back to his car.

He bought a *New York Times* at the airport and when he was safely on the T.C.A. 6 A.M. "early bird" to St. Louis, he started to read the paper, thoroughly, story by story.

And on page 32, he found a story that told him why two major Mafia figures were on their way to the Midwest to meet with an obscure college professor.

Already in St. Louis, Don Salvatore Massello was reading the same story which told how the television networks were sending representatives to Edgewood University where a conference had been called by Dr. William Westhead Wooley to announce "the greatest technological breakthrough in the history of television."

The conference was getting underway that night.

Don Salvatore swore softly under his breath. The story meant that he would have very little time to negotiate with Wooley before Grassione would have to be turned loose on the man. And if the television networks showed any interest in Wooley's invention, as they surely would, it would certainly drive Wooley's price up out of Don Salvatore's reach. And other people's involvement meant that the secret of Wooley's invention was just that much more vulnerable to public disclosure.

Don Salvatore snapped the paper closed and leaned forward to check in the rear-view mirror. Grassione's car, driven by that strange looking Oriental who had accompanied him, was still behind the Don's as they pulled into the closed boatyard and arrived at Massello's tied-up yacht.

He politely offered Grassione and his men the use of his yacht as their headquarters and home while in St. Louis, as custom required.

"No, Don Salvatore," Grassione said. "We're going straight to the campus to look it over for the hit."

"If there is a hit," Massello reminded him.

"Of course, Don Salvatore," Grassione said. "But if there is to be a hit, I want to know everything I can about this college and all, so we can do it and get out without trouble."

Massello nodded his approval as Grassione's car turned and drove off. On his way from the boatyard, Grassione sank deeper into the seat and thought that Don Salvatore was very bright, but he didn't know everything.

For instance, he didn't know that Grassione's uncle, Don Pietro Scubisci, had personally visited Grassione the night before to tell him that Don Salvatore seemed "to be getting too big for his own good" and that an accident to him would not be looked on unfavorably by the national council.

No. Don Salvatore didn't know everything. There would not be one hit; there would be two. And neither of them was a maybe.

Definite.

As definite as bang, bang.

Chapter Six

If God had created a human vessel for worry on earth, its name was Norman Belliveau. He had been born in France on D-Day and grew up in the United States to be the living embodiment of worry. He worried about how he looked, which was tall and thin with sunken cheeks and a hooked nose. He worried about how he dressed, which was after the fashion of college drama teachers: lousy.

He wore loud jackets and fuschia or purple or pink shirts, with an ascot. To keep up with the changing theatrical world, however, he wore levis and hush puppies.

But he usually bought a new pair of jeans after the first wash. Levis always faded and Norman thought faded Levis looked tacky. So now everyone on the Edgewood University campus knew when Norman was coming by the swish-swish-swish of his too new jeans.

Norman Belliveau inherited his worry from his mother who named him Norman because the allies landed in Normandy and she thought naming her son that would bring him good luck.

And then it didn't, and their home was destroyed by an erring artillery shell, and Norman's father killed by stepping on a forgotten land mine, she tried various other methods: stuffing rabbits' feet in Norman's pockets, throwing salt over his shoulder constantly, and not allowing him to step on cracks in her presence.

But nothing worked and Norman worried about that, but now he had more important things to worry about.

Like the rooms.

It was bad enough that Professor Wooley had gone ahead and scheduled the conference on some kind of technological breakthrough without telling anyone. That was bad enough. Suppose no one came? The university would be a laughing stock.

But people came. Oh, how they were coming, and where was Norman going to put them all?

This new interruption was the last straw. Imagine being dragged away from a very important classroom lecture to have to personally inform somebody that there was no more room. Hadn't he told the guard to allow nobody else in?

Norman worried about why guards never followed instructions. They had ignored his orders when that television reporter, Patti Shea, had shown up.

Norman had heard of her and her catty reports on the odd and unusual gatherings all over the world. He could not understand what she was doing at a technical conference in Missouri and he told her so.

"Just get me a room, will you, bub?" she said. "I've got a migraine you wouldn't believe."

She had rubbed a delicate hand on her forehead, highlighting her springy breasts under a tight yellow turtleneck. She let her right leg bend under her purple miniskirt and posed for an imaginary camera as "Woman in Pain."

Norman Belliveau checked the lists of representatives arriving and dormitory rooms still vacant. He stammered that there was very little room left.

"Oooh, that looks nice," said Patty, pointing to a small cottage with one hand while rubbing Belliveau's thigh with the other. She had to bear down to be felt through the stiff denim.

Norman stopped going through the lists.

"Uhhhh," he said, feeling lightheaded, "I don't see why we couldn't put you there ... I mean, uhhh, I wouldn't mind."

And he didn't really. After all, it was his cottage and if he wanted to lend it to somebody, why not? And the dorm rooms really weren't that bad. He could stay in one for just a few days, even with all that horrid music all night long and the dirty students.

But he had only one cottage to give and now he was called to the gate again, where the guard had been given strict orders to admit no one who did not have a room already.

What a waste of his time. If he wanted to do something besides teach his class, there were plenty of things he could do. He could go to the cafeteria and make sure that they could get the student's macaroni-and-cheese dinner out in time, to bring in brisket of beef for the university's guests.

Norman was worried that the beef brisket wouldn't thaw out in time. He worried that it might cook up dry. He worried that the delegates to the conference wouldn't like it.

He worried about his health when he saw the huge black limo parked just inside the gate.

He stopped a full twenty feet away, blinked, and stood staring.

Outside the car stood a Chinese, wearing a chauffeur's uniform, and a big ugly man in a suit that didn't seem to fit because of the lumps between his chest and his arms.

Norman Belliveau worried about whether to run or not.

The man froze him in place with a growl. "Are you Bellevue?" he asked.

Norman worried about whether he should correct the man's pronunciation. He just nodded.

The big man tapped the black back window which was sealed off from the outside world by a curtain.

Belliveau worried about getting his pension in fifteen more years.

The back door of the Fleetwood opened and Belliveau heard a song ring out:

"Meet George Jetson!"

A head followed the sound.

"His boy, Elroy!"

The face was impassive and the dark eyes under the neatly combed hair seemed to bore into Belliveau.

"Jane, his wife!"

The fading strains of a highly orchestrated "chopsticks" disappeared. The green glow that had illuminated one side of the man's face faded as he leaned out of the car, away from its built-in television set.

Arthur Grassione looked at Norman Belliveau and said simply: "You're going to find room for me and my men."

Norman worried whether the new guests would like the rooms he had picked for them.

Chapter Seven

Tuesday's Pub was not just any old bar.

When it had been called the St. Louis Tavern, it was any old bar. When it was the St. Louis Tavern it served the beer that made Milwaukee famous on tap to the bums that made St. Louis famous.

But then some smart cookie downtown figured that since it was near the train station and across the street from the Greyhound bus stop, and not far from the airport, the St. Louis Tavern was the perfect place to renovate into a modern watering hole.

So as the sodden regulars continued trying to see their gray futures in the golden liquid in their dusty glasses, the old interior was transformed into the smooth plastic decor of Tuesday's Pub.

The only problem was that it hadn't worked. The neighborhood had turned into a slum faster than the tavern could be turned into a cocktail lounge and now the owners were left with a joint, with a fancy name, new but ripped plastic seats and an even tougher clientele than the ones they had tried to chase.

When Dr. Harold Smith arrived, he was almost overcome by the pervasive stench of camaraderie that only dead drunks have for each other. Wood, urine, plastic, all combined their smells in an olfactory welcome, which was not shared by the people at the bar.

Standing inside the door, waiting for his eyes to adjust to the dark, Dr. Smith with his precisely creased gray suit, white shirt and regimental tie, and his gray two-suiter that was guaranteed to withstand a fall from the top of a twenty-story building, drew a lot of attention from the regulars of Tuesday's Pub.

"Hey, hey, look at the honkey," someone called from the bar.

"Woowee, he look like a professor. I bet he think he in the city museum."

"No," Smith said aloud. "Not a museum."

He walked past the bar to the back room, where he saw Remo and Chiun sitting at a table. Remo was counting ceiling tiles and Chiun was watching a dart game in progress.

Smith eased himself into an empty chair across from Remo, who continued to look at the ceiling.

"Nice places you bring me to," Smith said.

Remo still stared at the ceiling. Chiun nodded to Smith.

"Remo, it is Emperor Smith. Emperor Smith is here," he said.

66

Without looking down from the ceiling, Remo said "Did you bring the money?"

"Into this place?" Smith said.

"Don't weasel-word me," Remo said. "Have you got the money for my house?"

"I can get it in ten minutes," Smith said. "Now what is all this about a house?"

While Remo tried to explain, about how he was discontented even though perfect, Chiun turned and watched the dart game.

The board was an old-fashioned American dart board, a large pie divided up into twenty equal slices. Each wedge-shaped slice was cut up again into three arc-like pieces. The largest one, closest to the center of the board, counted one point; the next, red arc, counted two points, and the smallest arc, another white one on the outside of the board, counted three points.

The two men were playing baseball with each man taking turns throwing three darts at the sections of the board number one through nine.

A man with an electrified Afro was leaning forward over the shooting line, when he sensed Chiun's eyes on him, and he rocked back on his heels and turned to the aged Oriental.

"Whuffo you staring at me?" he demanded.

"I was just watching you throw those needles," Chiun said pleasantly.

The man nodded as if vindicated and turned back to the board.

"And wondering why you do not learn to do it correctly," Chiun said.

"Heh, heh," the man said. He looked at his playing partner who chuckled too, and explained to Chiun: "Willie's the best in the bar."

"Maybe the best in town," Willie said.

"Think how much better you would be if you knew what you were doing," Chiun said.

"Chiun," Remo said, "will you stop fooling around? The least you could do is pay attention to what we're talking about."

"I already have a house," Chiun said. "I'm sure that you and the emperor will make everything come out all right. I am just trying to help this awkward one. Willie."

Ting. Ting. Ting.

Formica chips flew on the table as the three wooden darts slammed through the covering and buried themselves in the wood beneath.

"There you go, old man, you so smart, you show me."

Remo reached over and pulled the three darts from the table. He snapped the pointed metal tips off each one and then tossed them back to Willie.

"Stop fooling around," Remo said. "Can't you see I'm buying a house? Why don't you go to the welfare office? Today's check day."

Remo turned back to Smith. "No house, no work, that's it, case closed," he said.

Smith shrugged. "You realize, of course, that your security will be greatly compromised by a house. That was part of the program in the first place, your continuing to move around, from place to place, so no one would be able to track you down. That's why you're not supposed to ever return to Folcroft."

"It's different now," Remo said. "Suppose somebody does track me down? What are they going to do?"

"Kill you," Smith said.

"Damn right, I kill you, honkey. You ruined one sweet set of darts on me," Willie said, approaching the table.

Remo shook his head at Smith. "Nobody can kill me," he said.

"I kill you, honkey," Willie shrieked. "Them was good darts."

Remo turned toward him. "Will you go away? Can't you see I'm talking business here?"

He turned back to Smith. "See, my safety's not a problem anymore, so all you've got to worry about is security for the organization. We'll do everything under a fake name."

Smith sighed and shrugged.

"So it's settled?" Remo said.

"I'm gonna settle you," Willie yelled.

Remo said, "Now I've been very nice with you, Willie, so far. Don't make me spoil my good record."

"Who gonna pay for my darts?" Willie's yelling had started to attract a crowd, as men, glasses in hand, moved away from the bar and toward the back room.

"Settled?" Remo asked Smith again.

Smith nodded.

Remo turned away. "I'll play you for your darts, Willie," he said.

"Give 'em here," he said.

Willie tossed the three tipless darts onto the table and Remo picked them up. It had been a dozen years or more since he had thrown darts, back when he had been a policeman on the Newark police force. He was pretty good then but now as he hefted the darts, he realized he had known nothing then. He had gotten pretty good at the game by making his mistakes consistent, not by learning to throw darts correctly.

"One inning," he said to Willie. "If you win, I'll give you fifty dollars for your darts."

"Twenty dollars," Smith said.

"I'll give you a hundred dollars for your darts if you win," Remo said. "And if I win, we just forget it."

"All right," Willie said, with a slow smile washing over his face. "Clarence, you go get some darts from the bar."

Three more brand-new wooden darts were brought to the back room. Willie looked them over then handed them toward Remo.

"You first," Remo said. "I want to see what I have to beat."

"Okay," Willie said. "I pick the inning. We shoot number four."

Willie leaned over the shooting line, and carefully threw the darts at the board. The first two landed in the red ring; the third in the outside white ring.

"That seven points," Willie said with a smile.

He pulled the darts from the board and handed them to Remo who remained sitting at the table, facing away from the board.

"That's all right," Remo said. "I'll use these."

"Hey, dummy, those darts ain't got no points on 'em," Willie said.

"Never you mind. I've got to beat seven?"

Without waiting for an answer, Remo twisted in his chair, to face the board, and then fired all three darts at once in a wide sweeping motion of his right hand.

Later on, people in Tuesday's Pub would say

the skinny white man threw the darts so fast no one could see them.

The three darts hit the heavy board with a thunk. Side by side in the white arc of the number four wedge, they hit, with such force that their snub noses smashed through the heavy cork and stopped only when they reached the wall behind.

"Nine points, I win; leave me alone," Remo said.

Willie looked at Remo, at the dart board, and at Remo again.

Remo stood up, along with Smith and Chiun, who whispered to Willie: "He is a showoff. It is better if the darts have points." Chiun looked down and took the three darts Willie had used from the young man's hand. He looked at the board once, then tossed all three darts with one easy motion of his right hand. The darts each buried themselves into the back end of one of the darts Remo had thrown. "Practice," Chiun said. "You will get better."

He turned to follow Remo and Smith. No one bothered them as they left Tuesday's Pub.

In the Volkswagen Smith had rented at the St. Louis Airport, he outlined their plan.

Smith would go on to the conference at Edgewood University and see what Dr. Wooley's "television breakthrough" was all about.

Remo and Chiun would wait for Smith until he contacted them.

He had arranged a place for them to stay.

In a hotel.

Chapter Eight

Whatever Dr. William Westhead Wooley had done, it had hit a nerve, and his simple technological conference had turned into an event.

Hundreds—from the media, from scientific foundations, from industry—babbled amidst the remnants of their fruit cup, broiled brisket of beef, and snow peas dinner.

The booze had been flowing since the welcoming cocktail party. Dr. Harold Smith had found himself standing next to a greasy-looking man who was escorted by a six-foot-four, two-hundred-fifty-pound goon type and an Oriental in a black suit, who made the color look like a social judgment. The man insisted upon talking to Doctor Smith about how NBC's second season wasn't as good as ABC's season and CBS didn't have anything on the air that was any good at all, not counting Rhoda and Archie Bunker, and if he had something to say about it, there'd be game shows at night, because that was how you found out how people really acted, by taking real people and waving money in front of them.

Doctor Smith was about to excuse himself when a hush fell over the cocktail party.

Patti Shea had appeared. The Queen of Television.

Men's mouths were loosely open; women's were tightly shut. She was wearing a maroon gown, severely cut and open to just above the navel. The color of the dress did more than make her straw-gold hair stand out. It picked it up and pushed it in the crowd's face.

Patti Shea sighed heavily, causing her breasts to rise which created a major seismic disturbance at the front of her dress. Several matronly ladies sat down.

Patti's right leg moved forward to walk into the room. Her dress clung to it momentarily, then her creamy leg appeared through a slit in the garment which reached up to the thigh.

As she moved into the room, everyone made a desperate attempt to take their eyes off her. One man blinked and sat down. Norman Belliveau was biting his lower lip so hard it bled. Another man tilted back and fanned himself.

Some whistled silently, some winked at their friends, but no one ignored her—not until Patti had taken her seat at a table in the front of the room and the room again lapsed into normal activity. Some kept looking. Her crossing of her right leg over her left sent the man on her right reeling and the man on her left painfully remembering not to stare, at the expert elbow-in-the-ribs urging of his wife, who had decided that the teased hair on which she had spent $35 that morning looked cheap.

Lee (Woody) Woodward, the head of college affairs, had risen hastily from his seat at the head table and started tapping on his glass, which no one could hear because Stanley Weinbaum, director of admissions, was busy shouting: "Sit down everybody. That means sit down."

As usual, no one paid any attention. Little by little, however, they began to drift toward their seats as plates of artificial vanilla, flavored chocolate, and fake strawberry ice creams were dropped off at their tables.

Woodward rose to deliver his opening address, one he had written himself, filled with choice tidbits about the little man of the business industry, the unsung praises they all deserved, and his fervent hope of the good write-up their respective presses would give Edgewood University when the lights went out.

He had trouble dealing with anything substantive because Dr. Wooley had belligerently refused to tell anyone anything about what technological breakthrough he had made in the field of television. He had insisted only that "everybody be ready for the plop to hit the fan."

Dr. Harold Smith drummed his fingers, sitting at a table in the rear. Get on with it, he said softly to himself.

Arthur Grassione sat across a table from Don Salvatore Massello, smiling gently at the St. Louis kingpin. Grassione was flanked by Vince Marino and Edward Leung, who kept stealing glances at their boss, hoping he would start eating his ice cream so they could begin eating theirs.

In the front of the slowly darkening room, Patti Shea felt two hands grab her legs. She stabbed one with a plastic fork, hearing a muffled groan to her right side. Then she carefully placed a dish of ice cream on her lap. The other hand, meeting no resistance, scuttled up her leg, then closed triumphantly on a melting slab of ice cream. It withdrew hastily.

Suddenly there was a gleam in the front of the room. It wavered in a multi-colored rectangular shape for a moment, then took form. The entire room stared at a bright, full-color motion picture of a countryside.

It was filled with oxen and working people. Then there was a tall young man working in a water-soaked field. He straightened and the audience saw a handsome Oriental face. The strong face looked back and laughed. Another face filled the screen, an old woman chattering away in another language. The face moved out of the picture and there was a small village with yelping dogs and little yellow children playing together happily. A few men talked to one side. Women walked along the path, smiling. They were thin and dirty, but the thinness was the well-fed muscle of a good diet, and the dirt was the refreshing soil of honest, heavy labor.

The image faded and then changed to a sunset. Seen over trees, it was full of golden promise, and peaceful, almost perfect.

The pictures continued on the high screen mounted on the wall behind the head table, pictures of an impossibly mellow happiness.

Suddenly a voice was heard over the buzzing noises.

"These are views of Vietnam, a Vietnam that none of us has ever known. One that probably no Vietnamese has known in the last twenty-five years. For this is a Vietnam of the imagination. The imagination of my nineteen-year-old adopted daughter."

The lights came back up. Standing to the side of the head table was Professor William Westhead Wooley. He pulled aside a small curtain, so the audience could see a teenaged Oriental girl, sitting in front of a television set. Her eyes were closed and she was smiling even with four discs attached to her throat and temples, leading by wires to the television set.

"Ladies and gentlemen, I am Dr. William Wooley. And this is the Dreamocizer. It takes your fantasies, your dreams, your hopes ... and plays them on your television, just as you envision them."

Silence filled the hall. Don Salvatore Massello leaned forward and looked at the images on the large screen behind the head table, images that were washed out and gray because of the brightened room lights. Arthur Grassione looked at the picture for a moment, then turned away and with a smirk, shared his view with Vince Marino that the device would never sell.

Patti Shea sipped in her breath.

Dr. Harold Smith looked around the room, whose silence was suddenly shattered by a laugh.

It came from the head table, from Lee (Woody) Woodward, the head of college affairs.

"Is that all?" he said, laughing. "Is that all?

Dreams? In full color? Is that all?" He laughed aloud, began to choke on his laughter and reached for a glass of water in front of his ice cream plate.

"Stereophonic sound is optional," Wooley said.

Woodward stopped choking and laughing. "Wooley," he said, "you brought all these people here for that? For a trick?"

The rest of the room was silent. People stared as if at a major highway accident, unable to do anything but sure that something should be done.

"What do you call this?" Wooley said politely, pointing to the overhead picture, which was a duplicate of the image of the small television screen in front of the Oriental girl.

"Hell. Ricidulously easy to put together a fake like that," Woodward said.

"Come up and try it," Wooley said.

Woodward wasn't about to have Edgewood University blamed for this farce. He rose from the table. "Wooley, I'm going to have your job."

"After tonight, it's yours," Wooley said. He tapped the Oriental girl on her tee-shirted shoulder. "Come on, Leen Forth. Time to come out."

She opened her almond eyes sadly, then smiled at Wooley, who gently removed the discs from her forehead and throat. As he did the picture disappeared and the television screen and the wall screen both went black.

Wooley held up the four discs with the black wires leading from them.

"This is all it takes," he told the audience, "to unleash your imagination."

He gestured for Woodward to step forward. Woodward sat in the chair vacated by the busty young Oriental girl and Wooley began to attach the discs to his head.

"It is not necessary to get them attached to any precise points," Wooley explained casually. "The temples and the throat, almost anywhere will do."

As he attached the last disc to Woodward's right temple, Wooley saw the man close his eyes tight. "No need to concentrate," Wooley said. "Just think the way you normally do. Think about your favorite fantasy."

He tightened the disc on Woodward's right temple with a slight twist that made the suction cup stick fast.

A picture began to appear on the screens and the people in the cafeteria leaned forward. Some giggled in anticipation.

On the screen came a woman's eyes. They were green and beautiful.

As more of the picture became clear, the woman's eyes widened with fear. Her nostrils flared and as her entire face came into focus, everyone saw a dark piece of wide friction tape stretched tightly across her mouth.

The audience hushed and the only sound in the room were the moans and the heavy breathing coming from the woman pictured on the large overhead screen. A small trickle of blood oozed from under a corner of the tape. The beads of sweat matched those that suddenly appeared on Woodward's own head.

His own mouth opened as everyone saw her delicate hands fill the screen. They were bound together with manacles that were chained through an iron ring on a hard concrete floor. The view on the screen enlarged and the audience could see the woman's miniskirted buttocks clench and unclench in pain.

Woodward's eyes widened as the audience saw the woman's young body come into view, its shapely legs tied apart to two more iron rings in the floor. Then everyone saw Lee Woodward enter the picture. He came toward the woman, his hand reaching down, clinging to the hem of her skirt.

With a roar, Lee (Woody) Woodward, Harvard '46, Columbia University School of Education, M.A., '48, Ph.D., '50, ripped the discs off his head and jumped to his feet. The image vanished from the screen. Woodward panted.

"Hey," said Stanley Weinbaum, director of admissions, "why'd you stop it? It was just getting good."

Woodward looked at the audience which looked at him, then glanced left and right, like a small animal trying to escape a forest fire. There was no escape. He looked back at Professor Wooley, a pleading anguished look on his face.

"As I said," Wooley explained coldly, "stereophonic sound is optional."

Wooley looked up at the crowd again. "This is the Dreamocizer, ladies and gentlemen. Tomorrow, I will be available at my home on campus to answer your questions."

He reached down to the television set and from its back snapped a small plastic box to which the four electrical leads were attached. Then he put his arm around the shoulder of the Oriental girl, and they left the cafeteria through a back door.

Woody Woodward still stood in silent panic before the audience, but no one looked at him. They were busy talking with each other. The room was abuzz with whispered conversations.

Patti Shea got quickly to her feet and, not worrying about her image, lifted her long dress and ran to find a telephone.

Massello nodded at Grassione who whispered instructions to Vince Marino. Marino and Leung got to their feet and ran across the floor, toward the door Dr. Wooley and the girl had just gone through.

Dr. Harold Smith watched all this and thought. He considered, for a flickering moment, the financial value of the Dreamocizer as an entertainment device, then rejected the whole question as being none of his business. But he instantly saw its value in the field of law enforcement and intelligence. No secret could ever be safe again. No one, no matter how well-trained, no matter how close-mouthed could be hooked up to that machine and not reveal what a clever questioner wanted him to reveal.

In full color.

With stereophonic sound an optional extra.

Chapter Nine

Revenge was sweet. It had been a long time coming for Dr. William Westhead Wooley, five long years since Lee (Woody) Woodward had gotten the position Wooley had wanted, as head of college affairs. Five years in which Woodward had browbeaten him and denigrated his work. Five years in which Woodward had taken every opportunity to criticize Wooley, to undercut him with university officials, five years of trying to make Wooley a laughing stock on the campus and off.

Wooley understood why Woodward acted that way. It was the age-old conflict between the administrator and the artist, between the technician and the inventor. Woodward had been jealous of Wooley's genius and had tried to drag him down into the intellectual gutter of Woodward's own brain.

Five long years.

And all of it was repaid tonight, in twenty seconds of televised fantasy.

Wooley could not contain a smile. His adopted daughter, Leen Forth, looked at him quizzically.

"What's so funny, Dad?" she said.

He shushed her by pressing his right index finger to her lips.

They sat in a darkened office upstairs from the cafeteria where the Dreamocizer had just been displayed. Downstairs, Wooley could hear the scuffling feet of men who had followed him from the cafeteria, wanting to talk to him, to be the first to try to buy the Dreamocizer from him. Perhaps even to try to steal it.

Unconsciously, he pulled the translator, the small device which was able to convert fantasy thoughts into television images, closer to his chest.

Let them all wait. A night of sleeping on what they had seen and tomorrow the offers would be that much higher, the deal that much sweeter.

Not only money but recognition. To be something, to be someone, the purpose that had directed Dr. William Westhead Wooley's entire life.

He didn't want his name in lights. But he wanted a table at the best restaurants at 7:45 o'clock on Saturday nights and he didn't want to wait. He wanted to be recognized and pointed out on the streets.

He wanted Pearl Bailey to point him out in the audience during curtain calls.

Was that too much to ask?

His wife had never understood and that was why she was now his ex-wife.

She couldn't understand the driven hour after

driven hour he had spent working on his invention—"tinkering" she called it. Why couldn't he just be content with being another professor at Edgewood U.? Why couldn't he enjoy his wife and their adopted daughter and their neat little house on campus and be like other people?

And he tried to tell her that teaching a course in "Technology of Cinema and Television" wasn't the way he wanted to spend his life. He tried to tell her about the students' experimental films—all nothing more than a series of arty ways to get their girlfriends to take off their clothes. That was all he saw day after day. Young girls taking off their clothes while the proud filmmaker exclaimed: "I experimented with the light sources."

Last term, the highlight had been three minutes of a young woman throwing up into a toilet while the camera zoomed in and out of her bloody private parts. When Wooley asked him what it was all about, the student filmmaker said it was a statement for legalized abortion.

And when Wooley asked what emotion he thought the film might evoke from an audience, the student went into a hysterical fifteen-minute dissertation on the holy integrity of the filmmaking process.

Before the sex films, there had been the musicals, all played in the nude. Before that, the students had done Macbeth as a western. Banjoes and all.

A man could go crazy from all that. And Wooley tried to explain to his wife, but she just wouldn't or couldn't understand, and then she was no longer Mrs. William Westhead Wooley. And Wooley took a shabby apartment in town where the prying eyes of his university fellows could not spy on his experiments with brainwaves.

And tonight, all the work had paid off, all the dreams were coming true.

Tonight, St. Louis, Missouri. Tomorrow, the world.

And the world could wait until tomorrow. The wait would just drive the price up.

Wooley and Leen Forth sat in the darkness until long after they no longer heard any sounds from the cafeteria. Then they sneaked quietly down the back stairs, walked across campus to Wooley's car, and got in for the drive to his St. Louis apartment.

When he opened his apartment door with a key, the first thing Wooley noticed was that the piles of dirt and laundry seemed to have grown since the last time he looked. He wished Janet Hawley hadn't just disappeared from his life. Not that she cleaned up his apartment—she would never have stooped so low—but she needled and nagged him into keeping it in some semblance of order.

He wondered why she never answered her telephone anymore.

Then Wooley noticed something else in the room. It was an odor, a rich pungent smell of tobacco smoke, the smell of a fine handmade cigar.

He stepped back toward the door, putting his arm around Leen Forth. But a lamp came on behind him and a soft gentle voice said: "It's good to see you, Doctor Wooley."

Wooley turned. Sitting on the couch was a dignified looking man with silver hair and piercing black eyes, wearing a dark pin-striped suit. Dr.

Wooley had been frightened when he had first realized someone was in the apartment but when he saw the man, the gentility and nobility of his fine-featured face, the smooth, warm smile he flashed toward Wooley and his daughter, Wooley's uneasiness vanished. He didn't know his visitor but obviously such a man meant no harm to Wooley or Leen Forth.

The man rose.

"I am pleased to meet you, Professor. I am Salvatore Massello."

"Remo, wake up." Smith's voice was like ice in the darkened hotel room.

He heard a snicker from Chiun, sleeping on his grass mat in the center of the floor. Then Remo's voice:

"You came up the steps, instead of using the elevator. Probably so you wouldn't make any noise. You tripped on the second step from the top of the landing. Just before you opened the door to this floor you coughed. You jingled in your pocket looking for the room key before you found out the door was open. And now you tell me, wake up. I ask you. How's somebody supposed to sleep if you keep making all this racket?"

"Do not abuse the emperor," Chiun told Remo in the dark. "He was very quiet."

"Yeah? Then why are you awake?"

"I heard your breathing change," Chiun said. "I thought perhaps you had been attacked by a flying hamburger. I was going to come to your rescue."

"Oh, blow it out your ears, Little Father," Remo said. "Well, what is it, Smitty?"

"Do you mind if I turn on a light? I don't like to talk to people I can't see."

"Learn to see in the dark," Remo said. "Oh, go ahead, turn on the light. My night's sleep is shot anyway."

When Smith turned on the light, Remo sat up on the couch and turned toward him. Like a slow puff of steam, Chiun rose from his sleeping mat until he was in a lotus position looking at Smith.

"Well, what is it?" Remo said.

"I thought you might want to look at a house," Smith said.

"At this hour? What real estate agent is showing houses at this hour?" Remo asked.

It wasn't really being shown by a real estate agent, Smith explained. Actually, the house wasn't even on the market yet. But it probably would be soon. And anyway, Smith just kind of wanted to get an idea of the type of house Remo wanted.

There were a lot of etceteras and Smith's car was rolling toward the guardhouse outside the main entrance to Edgewood University when Remo began to suspect he had been euchred.

The guard stepped out from the booth and waved the salmon-colored Volkswagen to a halt.

"We want to see Professor Wooley," Smith said.

"Sorry. I've got orders to admit no one but students until tomorrow."

Remo leaned out the window. "It's all right, officer," he said. "He's the head of a super-secret organization that safeguards our country's freedom from domestic insurrection."

"Remo. Please," Smith said.

"Hah?" the guard said.

"And I'm a secret assassin with more deaths on my hands that I can count. Deaths, that is, not hands," Remo said.

"Remo, stop," Smith said.

"Yeah, sure, buddy," the guard said, taking a step back toward the booth to be able to reach the phone.

"Wait, don't go," Remo said. "I'd like you to meet Chiun, reigning Master of Sinanju, and a man who could be a household word, if you could find a household interested in talking about kvetches."

"I think you all better just turn around and get out of here," the guard said. "I don't want any trouble."

He was about fifty years old with a beer belly so big it looked as if his wide leather belt would cut him in half if he exhaled suddenly. Remo suspected that the last "trouble" the man had dealt with had been an argument about overtime with the campus police union shop steward.

"You're not going to let us in? A master spy, a master assassin, and a master kvetch?" Remo said.

"G'wan, get outta here," the guard said.

"Too bad." When he woke up the next day, the guard wouldn't really remember much of the conversation; he'd just remember that the man in back didn't really seem to lean through the window, but the guard caught a flash of fingers and then felt a pinching sensation in his throat, and then he went to sleep.

Smith got out of the car, pulled the guard into the booth, and turned out the overhead light.

Remo settled into the back seat of the car, and then felt a pain in his right leg, as if it had been pierced with a dull stick.

"Owww," he said. "What'd you do that for, Chiun?"

"A kvetch is a scold," Chiun said. "A complainer. A whiner. A sniveler. I am not those things."

"Right, Chiun, right," Remo said. "Take the pain away."

Chiun tapped on Remo's right knee and the pain vanished as quickly as it had come.

"If I were a kvetch," Chiun said, "I would not treat you so lightly. I would complain and carp about your name-calling. I would remind you of all the years I have wasted on you, years spent trying to make something worthwhile out of a pale piece of pig's ear. I would scold you for frittering away what I have taught you in parlor tricks for fat men who stand in guard boxes. These things I would do if I were a kvetch. I would tell you about . . ."

Smith had slid back into the car and turned from the front seat and looked at the two men.

"What's the matter?" he said.

"Chiun is explaining how he's not a kvetch," Remo said. "He's certainly not complaining or carping."

"It is a minor thing, Emperor," Chiun said. "Drive on."

Before leaving the campus after the Dreamocizer demonstration, Smith had taken the precaution of driving by Wooley's house and now he was able to find the small brick and frame, ivy-covered building, nestled in a back corner of the large sprawling school grounds.

"Smitty," Remo said as they parked the car across a gravel-paved road from the house, "I know this is a put-on, so why don't you just tell us what you want?"

"This is Dr. Wooley's house," Smith said. "Tonight I saw his television invention. So did other people and I suspect he's going to be a target. I want you to make sure he stays alive until I can talk to him."

"Let's just go in and talk to him now," Remo said. "Then we can go home and let him die."

Smith shook his head. "Procedures," he said. "This may wind up costing a great deal of money. I can't do it until Folcroft's computers are opened by phone in the morning."

"All right," Remo said.

The three men crossed the street to Wooley's front door. Chiun paused on the top step, leaned his hands against the door, then turned to Smith and said: "He is not here. There is no one here."

"How can you tell?" Smith said.

"Vibrations," Remo said. "He's not here. Let's go home. To our hotel."

"No. We have to look inside. He may have been taken away by somebody. Or maybe he just isn't home yet."

Remo snapped the front door lock with a twisting push of his wrist.

There was no one in the house and there were no signs of a struggle. The beds had not been slept in.

"There has been no battle here," Chiun said. "Even the dust of the windowsills is at peace."

"Good," Smith said, and directed Remo and Chiun to wait in the house for Dr. Wooley and to protect him and his daughter until Smith could speak to them.

As Smith went out the door, Remo called to him:

"Smitty, when you're checking your computers for money in the morning, make sure they've got enough left over to buy a house."

When Patti Shea had run from the cafeteria and found a telephone, her instructions from the top network brass had been simple:

"Get that machine and get that professor. We don't care how."

She had spent the rest of the night at the house she had commandeered from Norman Belliveau, calling Dr. Wooley's home but there was never an answer.

After midnight, her own phone rang. It was New York calling. She turned the volume down on the television movie she was watching before answering.

Again her instructions from the network brass were simple and did not invite discussion.

"Promise him anything; we're sending somebody out there to help you."

When she hung up, Patti Shea shuddered. She knew what that meant. But why was the network so interested in Dr. Wooley's Dreamocizer?

She looked back at the flickering television picture. Even without sound, she recognized a Canadian who had made a fortune portraying American cowboys extolling the virtues of a dog food he fed his own dog Luke. And then she realized.

Commercial revenues in television were in the billions of dollars a year. And who would spend ten seconds watching a dog food commercial when they could own their own Dreamocizer, and romp in their own fantasy world?

In living color.

With stereophonic sound an optional extra.

Who would be left to watch "Patti Shea Under Cover" when their imagination could put her between the sheets.

She knew whom the network would send "to help" her and now, for the first time since she had been aware that television did those kinds of things, she looked forward to the help.

The cafeteria where the conference had been held was an anthill of scurrying people when Big Vince Marino and Edward Leung returned to the table at which Grassione and Massello sat, and shook their heads.

"He got away," Marino told Grassione.

"Assholes," Grassione snarled. "An old man and a young girl and you can't catch them. What the hell do I pay you for?"

"They vanished," Marino said, "into thin air. Remember ... like that quarterback on that Banacek show where he ran around end and ..."

Grassione's glare silenced him. "I saw the show. Maybe what I need is a Polack detective and not you two." He started to say more, then remembered Don Salvatore Massello was still at the table, and he shrugged toward the Don who smiled, and then rose to his feet.

"I think I will leave you now," Massello said. "Professor Wooley said he would be at home tomorrow morning. I will meet with him then, and then . . . well, we will see what we will see."

Grassione rose, waited until the Don extended his hand, then shook Massello's hand warmly.

"I understand, Don Salvatore," he said. "Nothing will be done until you approve."

Massello nodded, turned and left.

Grassione waited until the silver-haired man was out the door before he said to Marino, "Find out where that professor's house is and see if he's there. I'll be back at the room and you let me know."

When they returned to the room with another negative report, Grassione was no longer alone. Two men from St. Louis, who were not part of Massello's crime family, had joined him.

Grassione did not bother to introduce them to Marino and Leung.

"I want you two to go over to this Wooley's house and if you see anybody going in, you call me here and I'll tell you what to do."

He dismissed them with a wave of his hand and turned back to the television set, as if Marino and Leung were not even in the room.

Chapter Ten

"A man should not have to live like this." Don Salvatore Massello's voice was concerned and gracious, and the movement of his hand indicating Dr. Wooley's littered living room was the embodiment of all-encompassing pity.

"How did you find me here, Mr. Massello?" Wooley asked.

"I know a great deal about this city. What I do not know, I can find out."

Wooley stared at Massello, then turned to look at Leen Forth who stifled a yawn.

"Excuse me a moment," Wooley said and led Leen Forth into the equally cluttered bedroom.

"Is this your pad, Pop?" she asked.

Wooley nodded. "I've been using it to do research that I was afraid to leave around the house. Why don't you get some sleep?"

"Okay. Hey, we really blew their minds tonight, didn't we?"

Wooley put an arm around the shoulders of the girl who was almost as tall as he was.

"We sure did. Woodward's never going to be the same," he said.

"Yeah, that too," she said.

"And tomorrow we'll be rich."

A small frown crossed Leen Forth's face. "Even when we're rich, Pop, things are going to be the same, aren't they? I mean, it's you and me against the world?"

"It always was."

"Good," she said. "Good night. He looks like a nice man." She nodded her head toward the bedroom door.

"Yes, he does." Wooley kissed her good night, and went back into the living room.

Massello was still standing where Wooley had left him but when the professor returned Massello sank back into his seat on the couch.

"You don't remember me, Professor, do you?" he said.

Wooley looked hopelessly lost.

"We met, perhaps two years ago, at a dinner for Indochina refugees. I wouldn't expect you to remember just another businessman. There were many people there that night."

"Of course. Now I remember," Wooley lied.

"At any rate, I am a businessman and I'll get down to business. I was at the university tonight and I saw the demonstration of your . . ."

"Dreamocizer," Wooley filled in.

"Yes, of course. I want to buy all rights from you to manufacture and sell it—and of course you would be paid a generous percentage on the sale of each unit."

"I really don't think I'm up to talking business tonight," Wooley started.

"I understand. I'm sure it's been a long day for you. And before that, long years, perfecting your device. It is patented, isn't it?"

"Yes. A string of patents."

"Good," said Massello, making a mental note to have a search done the next day for all patents in Wooley's name. "Just so that you are not, as your daughter might say, ripped off."

"Not much chance of that. But as I said, I really didn't want to talk business tonight."

"There's just one problem, Professor. As I said, I'm in many businesses around the area and consequently hear many things. I understand that men have come here from out of state, whose only interest is in stealing your invention."

"They'd have to find it first," said Wooley.

"Of course. You would put it away safely." Massello shook his head. "But these are the kind of men who would not stop at anything to get from you your invention. From you . . . or from your daughter. They would stop at nothing."

"I'll just have to be careful."

"One cannot be careful enough. I hope this won't offend you, Professor, but I know that at times you entertained a visitor in this place. A Miss Hawley?"

"Yes?"

"You have not seen her in some time?"

"No, I haven't."

"You will not. Ever again."

Wooley sank back into the chair.

"I'm sorry, Professor. But I wanted you to know the type of men you are dealing with. These men from New York will stop at nothing."

Massello saw the pained look on Wooley's face and rose from the couch. He came to Wooley's seat and clapped a strong hand on the man's shoulders.

"Come, Professor. It is not as bad as all that. Forewarned is forearmed."

"But I know nothing of violence. I can't expose Leen Forth to those kinds of . . ."

"You won't have to," Massello said. "I have friends. They will know how to protect you and yours."

The warming clasp of Massello's hand on Wooley's shoulder gave the professor a surge of confidence, a feeling of power.

"You really think so?" he said.

"I swear it. On my mother's sacred heart," Massello said.

The two men Grassione had sent to stake out Professor Wooley's house had only started to phone in their report about the middle-aged man and the Oriental and . . .

"That's them," Grassione interrupted. "That's them. Now look, the old guy's invented some kind of a television gadget. I want you to get it."

"And what about him?"

"Do anything you want with him," Grassione said.

While the two men were in the telephone booth around the corner from Wooley's house, Doctor Smith had gone, leaving Remo and Chiun behind.

98

The two men walked back toward Wooley's small house.

"What kind of a television gadget?" the bigger man said.

"Who knows? We'll find out from this professor, before we pop him."

The two men were surprised to find the front door to Wooley's house open and even more surprised to find two men lying on the living-room floor.

The bigger man flicked on the light switch inside the door.

"All right, which one of you is Wooley?"

Remo rolled over and looked toward the two men. "Actually," he said, "Chiun's more woolly. I'm kind of wash-and-wear myself." He turned over again.

The men looked at Remo and at the tiny Oriental whose back was to them, then at each other.

"Where's the other guy who was here?" the big man said, taking a snubnosed .38 caliber revolver from a shoulder holster. "Hey. I'm talking to you."

"The other guy isn't woolly either," Remo said, still without turning. "He's more like green twill, the kind you get in work pants. Go away."

The big man walked to Remo and put his toe into Remo's shoulder. "A joker, hah?"

He pushed with his toe, but the shoulder didn't move. He pushed harder. The shoulder still didn't move, but the toe did. Toe, foot, leg, and man went toppling backwards, hitting heavily on the living-room floor.

Chiun rose as the man got up to a sitting position. The man aimed the revolver at Remo's back.

"What do you want, fella?" Remo asked.

"The television thing. Where is it?"

"It's over there," Remo said pointing to a 19-inch Silvertone console. "But don't bother turning it on. All the good shows are off."

"That's enough," the man said, as Chiun brushed by him. He began to squeeze on the trigger, and then he felt the gun being turned in his hand. The metal of the trigger was cold under his index finger, and there was nothing he could do to stop the finger from squeezing and the gun went off with a muffled thump, muffled by the gunman's head which Remo had jammed down into the muzzle.

The smaller man at the door had taken out a revolver too. He aimed it at Remo, then felt a stinging pain in the left side of his chest. He turned to his left and saw Chiun there, his face contorted in sorrow, and the man started to say something but no words would come out.

And Chiun pushed him with a long index finger and the man stumbled forward, then went headlong into the picture tube of the television set which broke with a loud crack and a swift sucking hiss of air.

"You broke the TV, Chiun," Remo said.

"No. He broke the television set," Chiun said.

"Now how are you going to watch *As the Planet Revolves* tomorrow?"

"I am always prepared. I brought my own set. It is in a trunk in my room. Please do something about these bodies."

Remo started to protest, realized it would be unavailing, and got lightly to his feet with a heavy sigh.

The sky was just beginning to brighten when Professor William Westhead Wooley and his daughter arrived back at their home on the Edgewood U. campus.

The two gunmen's bodies were stuffed into garbage pails behind the house when Wooley put his key into the unlocked door, turned and stepped into the living room with his daughter behind him, still rubbing sleep from her eyes.

Wooley saw Remo and Chiun sitting on the sofa.

"Dr. Wooley, I presume," Remo said.

"Who are you?" Wooley said. Leen Forth's eyes opened wide as she saw Chiun, then even wider as she saw the shattered front of the television set.

Wooley saw the set too. "You should have asked me," he said. "You wouldn't find anything in there."

"We didn't try to find anything in there," Remo said. "But the two men who came here to kill you thought they might."

"You still haven't answered my question. Who are you?"

"We've been sent here to make sure that nobody harms you until you talk to a certain man," Remo said.

"And that man is?"

"He'll tell you when he gets here," Remo said. "Now why don't you two just go about your business? Breakfast, whatever, we'll make sure nobody bothers you."

"You're too kind," Wooley said drily. In the kitchen, while he clanged milk and juice pitchers, he whispered to Leen Forth, "If anything happens

101

to me, or it looks like there's going to be any trouble, I want you to call the man we met tonight. Mr. Massello. Here's his number."

"I told you, he looked like a nice man," Leen Forth said.

Chapter Eleven

The line in front of Dr. Wooley's house grew as Wooley and Smith talked in the kitchen. In the living room, Remo practiced breathing and Chiun amused Leen Worth by showing her examples of Sinanju paper art—in which Chiun dropped an 8½ by 11 piece of paper from above his head, and then using his right hand as a blade slashed pieces out of the paper until, by the time it touched the floor, it had been hacked and cut into silhouettes of different animals.

Patriotism had closed on the first cup of decaffinated coffee, in the kitchen. Dr. Wooley had explained to Smith that he did not really give a damn about the potential applications of the Dreamocizer in both national security and law-enforcement work.

Now Smith was trying sociology.

"Do you have any idea what you could do for

our nation? The Dreamocizer would eliminate hate. Aggression."

"You mean why go out and kill niggers when you can do it at home on your own television?" Wooley asked.

"That's crude, Dr. Wooley, but that's more or less the idea, yes. Imagine its application in prisons, in mental hospitals," Smith said.

"You see, Dr. Smith, that's the problem. I don't want to imagine its use in any limited application. I think my invention should go to the public to use as it sees fit."

Smith tried simple avarice.

"I'll match any financial offer you receive," he said.

"Too late," Wooley said. "I've already given my handshake on a deal, and so that's that."

"You know," Smith said, "that there are people who will try to kill you for the Dreamocizer."

"I know that and I want to thank you for sending your two men here last night to protect me and Leen Forth. But I'm no longer afraid."

"There's a man here from New York. His name is Grassione," said Smith.

"Never heard of him."

"He's working for a man in St. Louis. Don Salv—"

"Come on, Doctor," Wooley interrupted. "I'm really not interested in all these horror stories, so if you'll just excuse me, I've got a class to teach today."

"Have it your own way," Smith said, rising from the table. "You're making a mistake, though."

"At least it'll be my mistake."

"One last thing. You don't keep the Dreamocizer in the house here, do you?"

Wooley shook his head.

"Good," said Smith. "And I'd suggest that you and your daughter no longer sleep here either."

"Thank you. I've arranged that."

Wooley watched as Smith left the kitchen and mumbled to himself, "Don't forget your soapbox next time."

Wooley waited until Smith, Remo, and Chiun had left through a back door before he stepped out on his front porch. Eighteen people were waiting for him.

"I'm sorry," Wooley said, "but I have reached a commercial agreement concerning the Dreamocizer. Therefore I will not be able to meet with you. I thank you for your interest and apologize for any inconvenience I may have caused you."

The eighteen persons were still groaning when Wooley stepped back inside the door of his house and locked the door from the inside.

"Leen Forth," he yelled, "I've got a class. I'm going to wash up."

"Terrific," came her voice from upstairs. "Knock 'em dead." She said something else but her voice was swallowed up by the roar of a super-loud stereo.

Wooley peeled off his shirt while walking into his bedroom in the back of the house. He opened the bathroom door and a blonde woman with big purple tinted glasses was rummaging through his medicine cabinet.

"Don't you have any aspirin in this place?" Patti Shea said.

Wooley stared at the twin peaks of her large

105

breasts that poked through the coarse fabric of her bright shirt. Flesh that gleamed so brightly it appeared to have been shined peeked from the V-shaped gap of her unbuttoned shirt top. Wooley closed the door behind him.

"No aspirin," he said. His voice caught in his throat.

"Oh, take it easy, Tarzan," Patti Shea said. "Let me do my speech and take off. I've got a migraine you wouldn't believe."

Her baby beautiful features pinched together behind her glasses and she pushed the palms of her hands against her forehead. "I've been standing out there for two hours," she said. "Now wait a minute, will you?"

Wooley sat on the yellow laundry hamper beside the door.

Patti Shea leaned against the sink and took a well-practiced deep breath. Her pain-wracked face turned, almost as if on cue, into an automatic smile.

"Yeah, I've got it now. Television has been around for almost four decades now and has advanced at nothing less than a phenomenal rate. Amazing, isn't it? A little box turning into a multi-billion-dollar industry. That's right. Billions. But it isn't really amazing, not when you consider the hard work, knowledge, and experience of the men and women involved in the television art."

She became even more earnest at this point, leaning in, threatening to attack him with her cleavage.

"All this can be yours," she said.

Wooley's head snapped up, but her eyes held only blank boredom.

"The whole world of television can be yours," she said. "Who better than television to handle your television device?"

Wooley sighed wistfully, then looked at her breasts again.

"Only we would have the background to know how best to produce, distribute, and sell your invention. Go with the best. Go with experience. Go with television! Now here's how to order."

She stopped short as if trying to call back the last sentence which was her peroration of a five-minute commercial she had filmed for an album of "Music That Made History."

Finally she shrugged. "To hell with it. You sure you've got no aspirin?"

"No aspirin," Wooley said.

"Okay. Where do you keep the Dreamocizer?"

"Hidden where no one can get at it."

"Who have you sold it to?"

"I'll release the details in a few days."

"You know I can go on the air and label your device a fraud, don't you?" Patti Shea said. She was no longer smiling or breathing deep.

"When it comes on the market, you'll be a laughing stock."

"I suppose you're right," she said. "You know the chances are you're going to be killed for your machine?"

"People keep telling me that. If that's so, why does everyone want it?"

"Want it? We want it to bury it. You realize what the Dreamocizer's going to do to commercial TV? To me?"

"Yes, I suppose it will. I hope you'll excuse me, I've got to shower," Wooley said.

"You need your back washed?" Patti Shea said, rubbing her index finger across his bare chest.

Wooley only smiled, afraid to hope, afraid to speak.

Patty Shea laughed. "If you live, you'll be rich enough to afford a valet. He'll wash your back. Toodle-oo."

She brushed by him and out of the bathroom. He heard her heavy wooden clogs clumping across the living-room floor, then he heard the front door open and slam.

By the time he had stripped and stepped into the shower, Wooley was glad that he had made his half-million-dollar deal with Mr. Massello. He was already tired of the bargaining and the badgering that masqueraded as business negotiations. No more. He trusted Massello and that was enough.

When Wooley left his home for the slow stroll across the campus to Fayerweather Hall where his morning lecture was being given, he was followed by Big Vince Marino.

Dr. Smith saw the big hulking man lumbering along behind Dr. Wooley, and turned to Remo and Chiun who sat next to him on a concrete slab bench.

"The man is insufferably stupid," Smith said. "But I think you and Chiun ought to protect him anyway. If we keep him alive long enough, maybe he'll change his mind."

Remo grunted. Chiun watched birds fly overhead.

Chapter Twelve

Patti Shea didn't need this crap.

Ever since she had parlayed seven weeks of newspaper experience and a set of limber hips into a career as a TV journalist, she had been fighting a continuous case of jet lag. The back-and-forths across the continent, across the oceans, had put her out of sync with whatever world she was living in, and she paid the price with non-stop migraine headaches that she could relieve only by popping pills like a Harvard law student the night before a big exam.

And the crummy assignments didn't help.

She suspected that she got every traveling job that came up in the network because her boss was jealous of her talent and fearful of his job and wanted her out of town. The fact was, though, that she got those jobs because her boss knew that the more annoyed she was, the nastier and more insulting her reporting would be and the public lapped up the image of Patti Shea, media's Grand Bitch.

But this hadn't even been a reporting job. Being told to go make an offer on the Dreamocizer to Dr. Wooley.

Crap.

Well, William Westhead Wooley had been a cleverer bastard than anyone at the network had given him credit for. He had made his deal and now he wanted to talk to no one.

So much for that. There was more than one way to skin a cat.

When she got back to the house she had taken over at the college, a young man was sitting at her kitchen table. He had light brown hair, parted in the middle, and he seemed more to be surrounded by, rather than wearing a large Army field jacket, sewn and patched in several places.

He was playing with a hand grenade which he occasionally tossed from side to side before his steel-rimmed eyeglasses.

Patti stared at him through tired eyes, then threw her arms around him.

"Well, if it isn't the world's thirty-fifth greatest assassin," she said.

"Thirty-third," said T.B. Donleavy. "Two others died last week."

He backed off from her embrace as if she were a side of beef. He was a vegetarian.

She discovered this when she offered him a portion of the bacon and eggs she cooked up for herself.

"No thanks," he said, breaking open his second pack of cigarettes of the day. "I'm a vegetarian."

110

As he lit the cigarette, he held the match close to the hand grenade he was still holding and Patti wanted to shriek.

"I never knew that," was all she said.

"When you're in my business, well, meat just doesn't look the same anymore."

Especially the way T.B. Donleavy carried out his business.

Patti Shea had first run across him when she was interviewing the wife of a convicted Mafia hit man. The wife, infuriated at her husband's jailing, had threatened to tell all she knew, but when Patti Shea arrived, the woman would not say a word. She just kept fondling a small greeting card that Patti Shea was able to see was signed only "T.B."

The wife's remains were uncovered three days later from the ashes of her governmentally protected building, along with the charred remains of three guards. The wife still clutched the small card in her blackened fist.

Patty Shea began to dig into the records of law enforcement agencies to try to find out who T.B. was. She discovered an Irish-American with notable credits. His education had begun on a trip home to Belfast where he became involved with the northern Ireland strife. Not on any particular side, just involved. His scorecard read five Catholics and seven Protestants, which did not include the twelve schoolchildren and four adults he got when he blew up a school to get to three visiting anti-IRA speakers.

Back in the states, he was in demand from people who appreciated his style and his impressive record. For every contract a kill. The only thing that kept him below the top rank of assassins was that for most of his kills there were no contracts.

There had been a case where Donleavy was supposed to eliminate another professional killer who had written a book on Mafia practices, and to frighten a young publisher who had expressed interest in handling the book.

T.B. waited until the two went to dinner at a French restaurant, to celebrate the New York *Post*'s wanting to serialize the book. Donleavy showed up outside the entrance to the restaurant with a painter's tarpaulin covering a large object on his back. He waited there for two hours, smoking cigarette after cigarette, stirring cans of paint that he had stacked on the sidewalk, just out of view of the restaurant's main window.

When the budding author opened the door to leave, Donleavy pulled the tarp off the .50 caliber machine gun mounted on his back and blew the front of the restaurant off.

He ripped the man in half, nearly cut off the publisher's leg, killed a bartender, two waitresses, and three customers, wounded seven others and caused $150,000 worth of damages to the restaurant. When the smoke cleared, T.B. had gone.

When asked later about the injury to the publisher whom he was only supposed to frighten, he said: "That's about as frightened as any man can get."

Patti Shea had followed the trail of T.B. Donleavy through Ireland, New York, San Francisco, and Chicago. When she finally got to him, it was in a restaurant on New York's West Side.

She mounted her courage and told him that she

had been trailing him because she was going to expose him. Donleavy laughed so loud and long, he almost choked on his V-8 juice.

"What's so funny?" she asked.

"You," he sputtered.

"What's so funny about me exposing you?"

"I work for your network," he said.

And he had. And still did.

And now he was here, in her borrowed kitchen, playing with a hand grenade and waiting for her to tell him the target.

Talking around a piece of bacon and a large hunk of gooey yellow yolk, Patti Shea described Wooley and said "He's got classes today. Right now. You can find him in the large lecture room in Fayerweather Hall."

T.B. was pulling the pin out of the hand grenade, then replacing it. Patti Shea watched his thin long fingers with fascination. Pin out, pin in, pin out, pin in.

"The hall has the college TV station in the cellar," she added as an afterthought.

"You think I'm going to do it as a TV special?" T.B. asked. He got up, slipped the grenade into his pocket, and started for the door.

"Hey," she called, bounding up after him. He turned from the door and she drew near, pressing her food-warmed body against him.

"You coming back afterwards?" she asked, holding on to the lapel of his Army jacket.

"Watch the hands," he said. "The grenade might go off."

Patti jumped back as if she had been touching a rattlesnake and Donleavy went out.

He walked casually across the campus to his

car. When he reached it, he was well into his second pack of cigarettes of the day. And then the murmurs began.

Just one at first, a soft one, as if a voice was being overheard from another room. Donleavy had heard the same thing when he handled his first killing for money.

As it grew nearer the time to do the actual killing, the voice grew louder. Donleavy heard it saying, then shouting, "Kill for me."

On his second contract, there were two voices. On his fourth contract, there were eight voices. He had accidentally killed five people on that contract. He knew the voices represented all the people he had killed.

Now the voices sounded like the Mormon Tabernacle Choir without the harmony. And T.B. Donleavy didn't mind. As a matter-of fact, he liked the company. Killing was a lonely occupation.

He sat on a bed of pine needles in the warm briskness of the May morning, smoking. Cigarette ashes fell on his jacket and he ignored it. Students passed him. Some waved to him, picking him as a student because of the Army jacket and the steel-rimmed glasses. He ignored the waves. He picked his nose.

He saw an old Oriental and a young man with thick wrists walk by, talking to a middle-aged man who looked as if he had been carved from the trunk of a citrus tree.

Donleavy thought nothing about them. The voices were getting louder.

He was into his third pack of Pall Malls when he got up and went to the car. Opening the unlocked door, he pulled something from under the front seat and put it under his coat. He heard his first coherent chant of "Kill for us."

He walked toward Fayerweather Hall as the chanting grew louder. He circled the hall twice, then walked through it twice, checking exit doors and counting class rooms.

The main lecture hall was on the first floor. One class had just left, and Donleavy walked through the empty room. It had a high ceiling but no windows. There were two side doors and two exit doors in the front on either side of the blackboard. T.B. walked around the hall. He counted the seats. There were 445. He sat down in the middle of the hall, taking a seat on the left aisle.

The first student showed up ten minutes later. Donleavy was on his fifty-fifth cigarette. As the room filled up, no one paid him any notice. The young face, cigarettes, steel rims, and Army jacket made him one of them.

Wooley showed up twenty minutes later. He was wearing a short-sleeved yellow shirt, open at the neck, with double knit blue slacks.

As Wooley came through one of the back exit doors the 300 students stood and cheered. None of them knew exactly why, but they had heard that Wooley last night had somehow embarrassed Lee (Woody) Woodward at a conference, and anybody who had done that rated a cheer.

Wooley looked as if the cheers were only his normal due upon entering a classroom. The lecture began, and Donleavy thought that Wooley was a pretty good instructor. Sharp facts peppered with personal observations and experience. Occasionally, a humorous anecdote to illustrate a

115

point. But after fifteen minutes, Donleavy could no longer hear. The chanting had grown too loud. All he could hear was "Kill for us."

He heard the voices. He saw Wooley standing in the front of the room. He felt the weight of the object under his jacket. Sweat appeared on his forehead. The saliva built up in his mouth and he swallowed it. He pulled on a pair of black leather gloves.

"Kill for us." Donleavy looked at his watch. "Kill for us." It was twenty-five minutes into the lecture. All the other classes in the building would have been started by now. "Kill for us." The hallways would probably be empty. "Kill for us."

Donleavy stood up in his seat. A few heads turned toward him, then looked away, toward one of the side doors. The faint buzz in the room vanished away into silence. Entering through one of the hall's side doors was Lee (Woody) Woodward, director of college affairs. His hair was a white thicket around his reddened face. His clothes were wrinkled and baggy. His pants were stained dark at the crotch.

T.B. Donleavy did not see him. He was walking down the aisle toward Wooley who was now writing on the blackboard. Donleavy heard a sound. He turned as the students yelled, and Lee (Woody) Woodward ran by him. Woodward pulled a pistol from his jacket pocket and shouted, "You bastard. You ruined me. You bastard."

As Wooley turned, Woodward raised his pistol to fire at him.

Donleavy saw the revolver in the man's arm and as the arm raised, Donleavy reached under his Army jacket, pulled out a medieval mace, and smashed it down across Woodward's arm. The revolver dropped harmlessly to the carpeted floor of the lecture hall. The students cheered, but choked on their cheer as Donleavy raised the mace up over his head and smashed it down, deep into Woodward's skull.

The look of gratitude on Wooley's face as Donleavy had saved him from the shooting changed into a look of horror. And then there was no look at all as the metal spikes on Donleavy's mace ripped off Wooley's face.

The first swing was right to left, splattering Wooley's face on the floor and left wall. The second swing was a vicious backhand stroke from left to right, pushing part of Wooley's head into a red spiraling arc, some splattering students in the first two rows.

The quick first swings held the body upright. The third and last swing was up over Donleavy's head and came whistling down to cleave Wooley's head. Bone and brain bubbled up onto the carpeted floor and over the mace which had become a semi-permanent fixture on the neck of the late William Westhead Wooley.

T.B. Donleavy left it there and ran out the nearest exit door. He had things to do now that the chanting had stopped.

He had just finished his third pack and he had to find some more cigarettes. Quick.

Chapter Thirteen

"Look," Remo said, "we'll protect this guy for you because you're going to buy me a house. But that's all. Just because you want us to. Not because this is important. This Wooley's invented a cartoon gadget is all. How the hell can you think that's important?"

"It's important," Smith said. He sat behind the wheel of his car, his hands clenching and unclenching on the wheel.

"Sure. Earth shattering," Remo said. "Like most of the other nonsense you get us involved in."

"I don't pretend to understand everything about it," Smith said. "But just for openers, it would be invaluable in police interrogations. A good questioner can find out any secret. Imagine its application in intelligence work. Those are for a start. And try this. This Dreamocizer could be the ultimate drug. Somebody takes drugs now, he's leaping off into the unknown. But with this machine, he can go right where he's always wanted to go and do whatever he's always wanted to do. I can see two hundred million people sitting in front of these damn things and never moving. Zombies."

Remo did not answer. He was thinking about what it would be like to live in a big wooden house with big grassy lawns and big brown trees.

Remo pictured himself lying down on his lawn. He was holding something. It was an acorn. Across from him was a squirrel. It looked at Remo quizzically. Then it looked at the acorn. And it was not afraid. It hopped forward then stopped. It was no more than five inches from Remo's hand. In his mind's eye, Remo could see that he could have snatched it up or broken it in half or smashed its head in, but he didn't. Not his squirrel. Not on his lawn. There was no need for violence. There were no secrets, no national security to worry about, no spies or madmen or scientists or assassins. No junkies, Mafia, government. No Smith.

Remo saw himself offering an acorn to the squirrel and the squirrel took it.

He heard a voice call in his imagination.

"Remo."

Remo turned, as the animal ran off with its prize, and saw her there, standing in the doorway of his house.

She was beautiful.

Remo didn't see what she was wearing. He did not see the color of her hair or her eyes.

He just saw her and she was beautiful.

She came down the lawn calling his name.

"Remo. Remo. Remo."

Remo rose to meet her.

"Remo."

She had Smith's face. The thin graying hair. The face that looked as if it were sucking a lemon. She was wearing a gray suit and a white shirt.

Remo shook his head, blinked, and was back on the campus of Edgewood University.

He stared at Smith who was now standing beside him, a worried look on his face.

"Remind me never to invite you to my house when you buy it for me," Remo said.

"Are you all right?" Smith asked.

"Fine. Can anybody use this Dreamocizer?"

"It is evil," Chiun said.

"Keep out of this," Remo said.

"It is evil," Chiun repeated. "Dreams are meant to be only visitors in one's life."

"You're a great one to say that," Remo said. "You and your soap operas."

"My daytime dramas are just that. Stories. Lovely poems. I live in the real world."

"And so do I," Remo said. "Smitty, I want that house. And I'll protect your Professor Wooley and I'll make sure the wrong people don't get his machine and I'll . . ."

"Hold," Chiun said. "We are co-equal partners. Yet you prattle on about what you will do. What will I do?"

Before Remo could tell Chiun that he would no doubt be busy finding new things to kvetch about, they heard the scream.

They turned toward the sound.

A wail of many voices rose, then passed like a

cloud. Then a young coed stumbled through the pine boughs.

Remo caught the girl just as she was falling face first onto the asphalt of the parking lot. She sank into his arms. He gently turned her over so her blank eyes stared upward. She whined softly, piteously.

"What happened?" he asked.

The girl looked through Remo, unable to focus her eyes.

"Blood," she said. "Blood everywhere. I heard the noises. I looked up . . . hit me in the face . . . wet, couldn't see. I wiped it off . . . felt ear, eye . . . blood . . . Poor Doctor Wooley."

She started to wail and Remo let her down gently and told Smith: "Wait here until I see what's happening."

He ran off between the trees. He heard loud shouting ahead of him now.

Chiun cradled the girl in his arms and touched her on the neck, then rubbed the back of her head. He looked up at Smith.

"She will forget now," he said.

On the other side of the stand of trees, Remo ran past stunned, stumbling students until he found the exit doors that led into Fayerweather Hall's main lecture auditorium.

He stood beside the blackboard staring at the huge pool of blood with the broken-headed corpse in the middle.

He recognized Wooley at once; the body of Lee (Woody) Woodward meant nothing to him.

The red sea of blood reached across both exit doors and was building up slightly in the small

122

declivity formed by the blackboard wall and the incline of the first row of seats.

Remo saw the blood circle around a pair of shoes. The shoes had feet in them, feet that led up to a boy, sitting in a seat, doing an excellent impersonation of advanced catatonia.

He was staring straight ahead and gently touching dried brown bloodstains on his face.

Teachers and students from other classes began to gather around the pool of blood. They stood staring at the corpses of Wooley and Woodward. Several threw up. Some moved around to get a better look, then all started talking at once.

"Did anyone call the police?"

"Yeah. No. I don't know."

"Who did it?"

"Some madman. Woodward tried to shoot old Wooley and this lunatic took off both their heads with that mace."

"Who was he?"

"Dunno. Army jacket, steel-rimmed glasses. Looked like us."

Remo moved outside, walking past huddled moaning shapes. One had thrown up and was trying not to again. Another youth, who couldn't take his eyes off the exit doors, was trying to comfort a girl who was weeping hysterically.

This wasn't a dream. The students who had seen the murders would never forget it; they wouldn't have to strap their heads to a television set to conjure up a fantasy of blood and death. They had seen it, had it dumped into their laps.

Remo walked back through the pine trees. Chiun and Smith were still crouching over the girl.

Before Smith could say anything, Remo said:

"Wooley's dead, Smitty."

"Who did it?"

"I don't know, but I'm going to find him. You can forget the house for awhile," Remo said. "This one's a freebie. Will she be all right?"

Chiun nodded.

"Then leave her and let's go. We've got work to do. So long, Smitty."

Leen Forth Wooley felt something pull at her. She took off her stereo headphones and tried to dig on the new vibrations.

But it was only someone banging on the front door of her house. Usually, she would ignore it because Wooley wasn't home, but the knocking seemed more insistent, faster, than one of her father's usual visitors.

She drifted slowly toward the door, remembering Wooley's injunction to be cautious.

"Who is it?" she said.

"Leen Forth," came a student's young sounding voice. "Your father's been killed."

"Oh, my god," Leen Forth cried and fell backward into the living room. She took a deep breath, then rose and went to the door.

"How did it happen?" she coolly asked the student there, an eighteen-year-old boy with a complexion like pizza and the insecurity of an unfed kitten.

"Murdered. Some maniac at Fayerweather Hall," the student said unfeelingly, then stopped when he saw the effect of his words on Leen Forth.

"Thank you," she said and slammed the door.

124

So they had gotten to him. All those people with their greed and their promises and their threats, and someone had gotten to William Westhead Wooley because the world was afraid of his genius and wanted to silence it.

Never. Not if she could help it.

She fished in the pocket of her jeans and found the scrap of paper, and dialed the telephone number.

"Yes, Mr. Massello, dead. Murdered. Yes, I know where it is. Yes, I'll be right there. Of course, I'll bring the machine."

Then Leen Forth Wooley hung up the phone and ran from her house toward safety. Toward the houseboat of her father's friend.

Don Salvatore Massello.

Chapter Fourteen

Remo and Chiun seemed hardly to be walking, yet they were covering ground as if on the dead run toward Professor Wooley's cottage.

"First we'll make sure that the girl is all right," Remo said. "Then we'll see if we can get the dream machine. I'll need your help."

"Why?" said Chiun.

"She's . . . well, Oriental."

"She is Vietnamese," Chiun said. "You know what I have told you about Vietnamese."

"Yeah, but she might trust you."

"Why? Because we look alike?" Chiun said.

"Well, some Orientals all do look alike," Remo said lamely.

"All you pigs' ears look alike and I would not trust any of you," Chiun said.

"Do it for the country then," Remo said.

"What country?"

"America."

"What has this country done for me?" Chiun said.

"Ask not what this country can do for you," Remo said. "Ask what you can do for this country."

"Did you just make that up?" Chiun asked.

"No. President Kennedy did."

"And where's he now?"

"I don't want to talk to you anymore," Remo said. "I'll handle it myself. Just like I do everything else."

"Good," Chiun said. "It is almost time."

"Almost time for what?" Remo asked.

"It is almost one o'clock. It is almost time for *The Gathering Clouds* to begin."

"Good luck," Remo said, as he dashed into Wooley's house, with Chiun close behind him.

Remo searched the house for Leen Forth while Chiun inspected the television set, broken by a gangster's head the night before, and determined that it was indeed broken beyond repair.

"She's not here," Remo said when he came back to the living room.

"This set is broken," Chiun said. "If it hadn't been for you . . . If I hadn't had to protect you, this would not have happened . . . this set would not be broken." He was working himself up from annoyance, through anger, to outrage.

"Too bad," Remo said.

"Heartless you are. Heartless."

"You find your stupid television set. That poor girl may be with that looney that killed her father. I've got to find them."

"Follow your nose," Chiun said. "Vietnamese smell funny."

Chiun went out on the porch and sat on the top step sadly, watching Remo race off across the well-watered grass of the campus.

It had been more than eight hours since Arthur Grassione had heard from the two men he had sent to Doctor Wooley's house to get the Dreamo-cizer and to dispose of Wooley.

Finally, he had sent Edward Leung there to see what had happened, and Leung had come back to report that the two men's bodies had been stuffed into garbage pails in the back of Wooley's house.

Leung's heart-shaped yellow face looked sad as he delivered the news.

"They were broken up badly," he said, and his tone of voice sent a chill through Grassione.

"Yeah, what happened to them?" he asked.

"One shot with his own gun. His skull blown away. The other one, no marks. As if he died of fright."

"Just like the others," Grassione said.

"What's others?" said big Vince Marino, stand-ing by the window of the second-floor apartment, looking out into the curved drive below.

"All those people we been losing. All over the country. Just like that. Shooting themselves. Scared to death. There's somebody doing some-thing to us." He looked up and caught a hint of a smile on Edward Leung's mouth.

"What are you smirking about, you goddam fisheating fortune-telling freak?"

"Nothing, sir," Leung said.

"You'd better talk, coolie."

129

Leung took a deep breath before speaking. Slowly he said, "I warned you of this. All of life ends in death and dreams."

"Aaaah, I don't want to hear your bullshit," Grassione said. "I shoulda left you in that gook carnival where I found you." He rose and walked to the window where he shouldered Marino out of the way. Looking down across the campus, he saw a thin man running. He had dark hair and even at this distance, Grassione could see his thick wrists. Something about him looked familiar. He must have seen him run before. But he had no time to puzzle about it because the telephone rang.

Don Salvatore Massello wished to speak to him.

"Were you responsible for what happened today in the lecture hall?" Massello asked.

"What? What happened?"

"Professor Wooley was murdered. And he had already agreed to our terms."

"Murdered?" said Grassione. "I didn't know anything about it. Who did it?"

"I don't know. I am told it was a barbarian act," Massello said, "so I assumed it was one of your people."

The insult flew so high above Grassione's head that he did not even hear its wings flap. "Not my men," he said. "We were staying away from Wooley until we heard from you. What about the machine?"

"I have been in contact with the professor's daughter. She is bringing me the machine. So all will work out all right," said Massello.

"Good. That's good," said Grassione with a heartiness he did not feel.

"Yes, it is," said Massello and without even the usual courtesies he hung up.

Grassione moved quickly to the door. "Let's go. Vince. You goddam Chink. Let's move it."

"Where are we going, boss?" Marino asked.

"We got to get over to Wooley's house. See if the girl's still there and try to get that machine. And then we've got a date with Don Salvatore Massello."

Twenty-one Edgewood University students who wore Army field jackets and steel-rimmed glasses were in their rooms all over the campus dormitory area when they were visited by a dark-eyed man with thick wrists who put an index finger, like a railroad spike, into their shoulder muscles and growled:

"Did you kill Wooley?"

None of them had and they were all glad because the momentary pain was so excruciating that they would have admitted the murder, they would have confessed to the slaying of Archduke Ferdinand at Sarajevo, even to the ultimate sin of having voted Republican, if that's what it took to make the pain stop.

But the pain stopped as quickly as it had come and before they could react the thick-wristed man was out the door.

Remo was out of leads and he was about to return to Wooley's cottage where Chiun was waiting, when he ran across a man walking back and forth on the sidewalk, wringing his hands together as if they contained an invisible dishcloth.

"Oh, my god," he said. "Oh, my god. What will

131

people think of us? Who'll ever enroll again at Edgewood? What are we going to do?"

Norman Belliveau looked skyward as if demanding an immediate reply from God and shouted: "What are we going to do?"

"Stop acting silly," Remo said.

Belliveau postponed his confrontation with God long enough to look down and see Remo.

"I'm looking for a man in an Army field jacket," Remo said. "A young man. Steel-rimmed glasses. You see anybody like that?"

"Dozens of them. Hundreds of them. All over the campus. Making us a laughing-stock. Not caring about the sanctity of the educational process."

"I don't think this one's a student," Remo said.

"No. Wait. I saw somebody like that this morning. He asked me for directions to my place to see Patti Shea. He couldn't be a student if he didn't know where I lived."

"Good thinking," said Remo. "Where do you live?"

"Over there," Norman Belliveau said, pointing. "You're not a student, are you?"

"No," said Remo and he moved away, leaving Norman Belliveau to worry about why all these non-students were on campus.

The door was unlocked and open and Remo walked right in. The back bedroom door was locked and as Remo pushed against it, he heard a woman's voice from inside.

"You've come to kill me, haven't you?"

"What?" Remo said.

"Come in. Come in. I've been waiting for you." Patti Shea pulled open the door and stood before Remo. She was dressed in a one-piece black

132

leather swimsuit cut down to her belly button and fastened by black leather thongs tied across the V-front, shoelace style. Her long curved legs were fully visible because the sides of the suit were cut up almost to the waist.

"Who are you?" she said.

"Where is he?" Remo said.

"You look like you'd punish me," she said. She moved back into the room and plopped down on the couch which was covered with wide leather belts, handcuffs, and pieces of rope. She hit herself lightly on the wrist with a black whip, waiting.

"Well? Wouldn't you punish me?" she said.

Remo stared at the rest of the room. It looked like a museum of sado-masochism. Shackles and manacles of all kinds lined the bed and furniture. Stockings and ripped pieces of cloth hung out of half-opened drawers. Silk ties were draped over the doorknob of the closet. Feathers and red rubber balls were strewn on the top of the dresser.

Remo imagined there were rose thorns lining the shower stall and metal studs on the inside of the closet.

"I'm looking for a man," Remo said. "Army jacket, steel-rimmed glasses."

"I won't tell you," she said. "I won't. You can just try to beat it out of me."

She closed her eyes and threw herself back across the couch with one arm flung out toward the floor, the other, palm up, on her forehead. Her long legs stretched out full-length on the sofa, exposing her entire body to whatever cruel, painful thing this stranger might plan to inflict on her.

"Listen, freakie," Remo said. "I don't have time to play in your dirty little sandbox, so where is he? The one who was here this morning for you."

Patti Shea opened one eye and looked at Remo. There was a look in his eyes that ruled out lying.

"Oh, crap," she said and sat up. "You're not going to do anything, are you?" She shook her head, agreeing with herself. Her breasts kept time with her head movements. "You're looking for T.B. I set this up for him. It relaxes him after a job."

"So where is he?"

"He'll be here. He'll be here," she said. "But we wouldn't have to waste the time, you know."

"Sorry. The Good Ship Lollipop will have to sail without me."

"Come on," she said in exasperation.

"No."

"Please?"

Remo shook his head.

"I know. There's something missing, right? I knew it."

She ran to the closet and pulled it open. Remo was right. There was a blanket of studs covering the wall. She leaned down and with her rear aimed directly to Remo's face, started pulling out whips.

"Just tell me what you need," she yelled, as whips and chains flew out of the closet and landed on the floor behind her.

"Just my hands," Remo said. "Just my hands."

He turned as he heard the front door open, and T.B. Donleavy walked in, his Army field jacket coated with blood, dried specks of brown dotting his glasses and face.

Patti followed Remo into the living room as Donleavy said, "Who are you?"

"T.B., this is . . . what'd you say your name was?" Patti Shea asked Remo.

"I didn't say."

"This is T.B. Donleavy, thirty-fifth greatest assassin in the world," Patti said.

"Thirty-third," said Donleavy.

"My name's Remo. I'm the second greatest, and you're dead."

"Hold on, pal," Donleavy said. He felt a twinge of fear in his stomach. And the voices were sounding up again. But they were saying something different. What was it?

Remo turned to Patti. "You people hired him to kill Wooley so his Dreamocizer wouldn't put you all out of business, right?"

"You got it," Patti said. "Now let's get it on."

"Too late," Remo said. "Too late for both of you."

Donleavy could understand the voices now. They weren't saying "Kill for us." They were saying "Come to us."

"I'm leaving," Donleavy said, trying not to shout over the volume in his brain.

From his jacket pocket, Donleavy pulled the hand grenade and with his teeth pulled the pin from it.

"I'm leaving now. If you're smart, you won't try to interfere," he said. He held the grenade in front of him as if it were a switchblade knife.

"Come to us. Come to us." The voices were shouting now, thundering inside his head, a rising roaring crescendo of noise that ripped at his brain like hammers. "Stop," he screamed. "Stop."

He tossed the grenade onto the floor toward Remo's feet and turned to race toward the front door. But the dark-eyed man with thick wrists was there, waiting for him, and T.B. Donleavy felt himself being dragged back into the room, his protesting kicks ineffectual, not even slowing him down and then his mouth was being opened, and he felt the taste of cold metal.

Remo jammed the grenade deep into Donleavy's mouth. Donleavy could feel the vibrations atop his tongue as the deadly little bomb's spring action wore down to explosion time. He tried to scream. But he could not hear himself over the voices, yelling "Come to us. Come to us."

And then he heard Remo say, "Here, give your honey a great big kiss," and he felt his face being pressed against Patti Shea's, her so usually soft lips turned by tension into strips of sinew, and the madman's hand was on the back of his head, holding him and Patti Shea together, mouth to mouth, and there was one final scream by the chorus:

"Come to us."

And T.B. Donleavy blew up.

The explosion blasted off the top of his head, but the tough human skull resisted the destruction just long enough for the rest of the blast to be diffused forward, where it blew off Patti Shea's face, and downward through Donleavy's body.

Remo matched the velocity of the exploding grenade in an outward push he performed after his brain pre-registered the original flash.

But the blast running down through Donleavy's

body ignited, in a whoosh of fire, a pack of plastic explosive the Irish assassin had strapped around his waist.

A split-second after the first blast, the gelignite exploded with a muffled thump and Remo, unprepared for that concussion, was tossed across the room and against a wall.

Before he sank in a great expanse of dark, Remo thought, Now I'll never get that house.

And then he thought: That's the biz, sweetheart.

Chapter Fifteen

When the black limousine rolled up, Chiun was still sitting on the front steps of Dr. Wooley's house, contemplating the perfidy of an America where one could not find a television set when he needed one.

There were post office boxes on almost every corner, and who would want to commit anything to paper in this savage land? There were telephone booths everywhere and who would want to speak to an American?

But let it be something important, like one of the beautiful daytime dramas, and try to find a television set.

Even the Master of Sinanju was helpless in front of the face of such stupidity. But was that not always the way? Stupidity was invincible, else why had it been the single most significant characteristic of all man's recorded history?

Chiun watched as the big man and the Oriental got quickly out of the car and walked toward Wooley's house. The Oriental was Chinese and Chiun spat into the aspidastras of the garden. Remo would hear about this. Chiun's air space was being befouled by a Chinese, and the Master of Sinanju did not have a television set upon which to watch his daytime dramas, and where was Remo? Out someplace fooling around. He would hear about this, for certain.

Vince Marino and Edward Leung stopped in front of Chiun.

"Is there anyone in there?" Marino said.

But Chiun did not answer. He had heard something. He rose smoothly to his feet and brushed past the two men, moving quickly toward the back of the black limousine. The sound was familiar.

Chiun pulled open the back door.

It was. It was.

There was a television set built into the back of the front seat. A swarthy man sat in the back of the limousine watching the television which was tuned to a commercial for a driving school that was so good its owner was always pictured riding a bicycle, roller-skating, or skiing, but never behind the wheel of a car.

"What are you watching?" Chiun said as he slid into the back seat.

"Who are you?" said Arthur Grassione.

"The Master of Sinanju," Chiun replied. "What are you watching?"

Before Grassione could answer, the commercial faded and the green-tinted set blared forth into the music of *The Divorce Game,* a show in which

140

newly divorced couples were the contestants and by telling stories of how their partners had mistreated them during marriage tried to win the support of the studio audience. The show had come under attack in its first year when a watchdog group had claimed many of the contestants were not really divorced, but the show's producers had pulled through by pointing out that no one had appeared on the show without being divorced within the next ninety days.

"You are not going to watch this drivel, are you?" Chiun demanded.

"I never miss it," Grassione said.

"Today, miss it," Chiun said. He flicked out his hand and changed the channel until the familiar organ music theme of *The Gathering Clouds* filled the back seat of the car, and Chiun sat back contentedly in the Cadillac's luxurious velour seats to watch.

"I will explain to you what it is all about," Chiun said. "You see, there is this doctor . . ."

Leen Forth Wooley pulled through the open gate of the boatyard and drove slowly over the rutted road toward the large white yacht in the back.

She parked in front of it and saw Mr. Massello standing on the main deck, smiling down at her. He walked toward the gangplank to come meet her.

She felt a feeling of relief at finally meeting a friend.

Leen Forth turned off the car's motor, and then reached under the dashboard for what appeared to be the car's stereo tape-player. It snapped loose at both sides, a small plastic box filled with transistors and hand-wired circuits. She clutched the Dreamocizer control box to her breasts and stepped out of the car to meet her father's friend, Don Salvatore Massello.

Chapter Sixteen

Remo saw happy children laughing, big warm houses and lovely women secretly smiling. But they kept bursting into flame. And what was worse, they didn't seem to notice. The children kept on laughing, the women smiling.

Remo woke up. He was sitting on a hot floor in the middle of a roaring inferno. One of his legs was stretched full length and the trousers had been burned through by drops of the explosive gelignite. He pulled the leg up to his other which was bent to his chest.

The room crackled with flames.

Outside, the entire fire department of Edgewood University—two men and a truck—had arrived to fight the blaze. They had battled for ten heroic minutes until St. Louis had sent in more equipment and trained firemen, whose technique in fighting fires was a little more sophisticated than pumping in enough water to launch Noah's Ark. The Edgewood firemen immediately began to drift off to talk to the Edgewood police about the terrible violence on campus.

Editorial staff members of the *Edgewood Quill* were at the fire scene, trying to sell copies of their mimeographed special edition on the violence, which reported that although Wooley and Woodward were dead, "there have been no reports thus far of student injuries. All's well that ends well."

The St. Louis Fire Department fought on for five more minutes, then the battalion chief in charge gave up on the house. He ordered his men to just keep it "wetted down" so that embers and sparks could not fly off and imperil any other nearby buildings.

"Let it burn out," he said.

"Suppose someone's in there," a fire captain asked.

"Nobody's alive in there," the battalion chief said and went over to buy a copy of the *Edgewood Quill* to look at until the photographers arrived at which time he would run back to the equipment and help his men haul hose.

Remo felt the heat blast at his body and the heavy hot air singe his lungs when he breathed.

He rolled onto his stomach to be closer to the floor and slowed his breathing to reject any smoke that might find its way into his lungs. He raised his body temperature so that he would not feel the heat so intensely.

He looked around. He was in the center of the room, surrounded by flames. The walls and ceiling were burning, and the carpeted floor and the wood underneath had caught fire and the flames

144

were now marching inexorably across Norman Belliveau's tweed pile carpet, $7.95 a square yard including installation, toward him.

He looked for a break in the flames but there was none. He moved himself into a crouch and then did what he thought he would never do. He ran.

He ran into his own mind. He could feel the flames lapping at his legs, and then in his mind, he moved into a room and he closed the door behind him.

The heat that singed his legs no longer hurt. He could breathe.

He thought he heard Chiun's voice and he yelled, "Get me out of here."

"Who are you?" Chiun said.

"Get me out of here. Save your silly games for later."

"If you were a baby I would carry you out," Chiun's voice said in that secret room in Remo's mind. "But you are not a baby. Who are you?"

"I am Remo Williams," Remo said.

"Not good enough," Chiun said.

Remo didn't want this to be hard. He wanted to be human and simple.

Now he could see Chiun. The ancient Oriental stood in a ceremonial white robe across the room from Remo. "Who are you?" he repeated. His voice seemed to be filtered through a tunnel because it resounded with echoes.

"I'm Remo Williams. I'm a Master of Sinanju," Remo yelled. He felt tears coming from his eyes. They sizzled and disappeared before dropping halfway down his cheeks.

Chiun's face grew cold, almost angry. Remo

opened his eyes and Chiun's face vanished. All Remo could see was flames. He closed his eyes again and Chiun's face demanded, "Yes, but who are you?"

And, in his mind, Remo stood and said, "I am created Shiva, the Destroyer, death, the shatterer of worlds. The dead night tiger made whole by the Master of Sinanju."

"Then walk out," Chiun said.

Remo stood and was back in the burning house. The flames engulfed him. The building shuddered, the flames seemed to roar in triumph.

But it could not match the roar in Remo's mind, the roar of realization and rebirth.

He ran forward through the flames, strongly breathing out, willing the flames away from his face and his eyes. It took only a split second to pass through the flames to a window and then roll through the window out onto the grass. He gulped clean fresh air, barely tainted by the smoke from the inferno behind him.

A fireman saw him come through the window and dropped his hose.

Remo smiled and waved.

The fireman said dumbly, "Your back's on fire."

"Thanks, pal," Remo said, and he spun around, a dervish motion so fast that it created a partial vacuum of thin air around him and the flames on his clothing sucked out and died.

"Take your time," Remo told the fireman. "Everyone else in there is dead."

Before the fireman could speak, Remo was running off from the house, across the greensward toward Professor Wooley's home.

He saw Chiun sitting on the grass in front of Wooley's house, his feet and legs crossed in the lotus position, his eyes closed, his long-nailed fingers bridged in front of him.

He came up close to the old Korean and said softly, "Chiun."

Chiun's eyes opened as if the lids had been pulled apart by springs. When he saw Remo there was just a flicker of approval.

"Thank you," Remo said.

"You look like something the cat dragged in," Chiun said.

"Thank you," Remo said.

"And you smell bad," Chiun said.

"Thank you," Remo said.

"If I hadn't met a nice man, I would have missed *The Gathering Clouds*. But do you care?

"Thank you," Remo said.

"What is this silly prattling?" Chiun asked.

"Thank you," Remo said.

"Aaaaah," said Chiun in disgust. He rose smoothly to his feet and walked a few steps away. He stopped, his back still to Remo and said:

"You're welcome. But the next time you get out of fires by yourself."

Chapter Seventeen

When Big Vince Marino and Edward Leung had found no trace of either Leen Forth Wooley or the Dreamocizer in Professor Wooley's house, Arthur Grassione had wanted to leave immediately for Don Salvatore Massello's boat.

But he couldn't.

The ancient Oriental who had taken over most of the back seat of Grassione's limousine had made that very clear.

"Just a little longer," he had said.

"And then it'll be over?" Grassione asked.

"Yes. And then there is *Search for Yesterday* and *Private Sanitarium* and *The Young and the Foolish* and *Hours of Our Sorrow* and finally Rad Rex starring as Dr. Whitlow Wyatt, noted surgeon, in *As the Planet Revolves.*"

"That'll take all day. I can't wait for all that crap," Grassione said. He looked to the front of the car and Big Vince Marino turned around on the seat, ready to help Grassione if he needed it.

"What?" Chiun said. "You would leave before ~~seeing~~ *As the Planet Revolves*? Starring Rad Rex?"

"You're damned right," Grassione said, but the old man did not answer because the commercials had ended and *The Gathering Clouds* had started again.

Grassione was ready to tell Marino to chase the old man from the car when there was a loud thump, as if there had been an explosion nearby.

The old Oriental sat bolt upright on the car seat. He closed his eyes as if concentrating, then pushed open the door.

"I would like to stay with you to watch our daytime dramas," he said, "but my child needs me."

"Yeah, right," Grassione said. "We always gotta take care of our kids."

"Isn't it true?" Chiun said, and then he was gone from the car, and Grassione, without looking back, motioned Marino to drive off. If it had been an explosion, he didn't want to be on campus when the police arrived to investigate.

On the way to the boatyard, Grassione explained his plans to Leung and Marion. They would kill Massello, kill Leen Forth, and take Wooley's Dreamocizer back to Uncle Pietro in New York.

He rubbed his hands in anticipation. "It'll be a good day's work."

"Sure will, boss," Marino chuckled. "Sure will."

Edward Leung said nothing.

A guard stood at the gate to the boatyard when

150

the black limousine pulled up. He looked into the back seat where Grassione was watching a rerun of *Death Valley Days.*

"Hello, Mr. Grassione," he said.

"Hi, kid," Grassione said.

"Don Salvatore's expecting you. Go right on in."

Grassione winked and waved. Throughout the entire conversation, he had not taken his eyes off the television set.

Leung drove slowly forward over the bumpy rutted road and Grassione told the two men what to do.

"I'll take care of Don Salvatore," he said. "You be hanging around and when you hear the shot, then you take care of his men. Do it quick and do it right. You understand?"

"Right, boss," Marino said.

"What about you, Charlie Chan?" Grassione asked.

"Whatever you say," Leung said sullenly.

Grassione left Leung and Marino on the deck talking to Massello's two bodyguards as he went down the steps into the body of the ship.

Don Salvatore was sitting in a lounge big enough to be a restaurant's dining room when Grassione entered. Seated on a chair across from Massello was Leen Forth. She was crying.

On a coffee table between them was a small plastic box, the size of a large dictionary, crammed with wires and transistors.

"You got it," Grassione said.

Massello shushed him with a slight upward wave of his right hand. He was wearing a silken smoking jacket. He rose and said, "Leen Forth, this is Mr. Grassione, a businesss associate. Arthur, this is Leen Forth Wooley. She has just suffered a terrible tragedy. Her father passed away today."

The girl stood up and turned to Grassione. There were tears in the angled eyes, that ran gently down her round cheeks. Grassione had not noticed the other night how beautiful the girl was.

"Sorry about your father," he mumbled.

"Thank you," she said. She lowered her eyes.

"Leen Forth," Masselo said, putting a fatherly arm around the girl's shoulders. "Why don't you go up and walk on deck? Arthur and I will only be a few moments. The air will do you good."

Dully, like a battery-powered doll that was running down, Leen Forth nodded and shuffled past Grassione. He watched her behind approvingly as she passed through the door toward the stairs.

Massello waited until the door was closed before he said to Grassione: "Success. We have it. And the girl will do anything I say."

"Anything?" Grassione said with a lift of his eyebrows.

"Do not be vulgar, Arthur. She is little more than a child."

"Yeah, but you know how them gooks are. They start when they're ten, eleven years old."

Massello took a cigar from a pearl-inlaid box and lit it with a wood-encased butane lighter whose color matched the deep rich paneling of the walls.

"Yes," he said exhaling a puff of smoke. "But we have other things to do than to discuss the sexual customs of the Orient. I suppose you'll be returning now to New York."

Grassione nodded. He turned away to look at the room.

"Your Uncle Pietro will be very happy," Massello said. "We will pay less for the device than we expected."

"Much less," said Grassione. He snaked his hand under his jacket and wheeled on Salvatore Massello. "Much less," he repeated.

Massello coolly took another puff on his cigar before nodding toward the automatic in Grassione's hand.

"What is this, Arthur?"

"Uncle Pietro sends his love, Don Salvatore. Take it with you to hell."

Grassione squeezed the trigger once. The heavy .45 slug kicked into Massello's body and seemed to push him back away from his cigar which dropped onto the table. The man hit the wall with a heavy thud, then began to sink down into a sitting position.

"You fool," he gasped.

Grassione fired again, into Massello's face, and the silver-haired man spoke no more.

From the deck, Grassione heard the answering sounds of gunfire. A quick flurry and then it was over, as suddenly as it had started.

Grassione walked to the coffee table and picked up Massello's cigar and puffed on it. No sense wasting a good cigar.

He looked down at the Dreamocizer, thought of the Oriental girl on deck, stubbed the cigar out in the ashtray and walked to the door.

Marino and Leung had shot Massello's two

bodyguards as they started toward the stairs leading down to the lounge from which they had heard the two gunshots.

As Marino toed the bodies to make sure they were dead, Edward Leung turned and saw Leen Forth staring at him, her eyes shocked wide, and he made a decision.

He ran along the deck, grabbed the girl by the arm, and ran to the bow of the ship.

Behind him, he heard Marino yell.

He kept running and just as he and the girl ducked into a door at the bow of the ship, he heard a shot splinter the wood over his head.

Now the two sat on the cold tile of the shower floor in the crew's locker room.

"You must be quiet," Leung whispered. "Grassione is an evil man and would kill you. We will wait till dark and then escape."

She just stared at him with her big brown questioning eyes, then surrendered with a sob and threw herself into Leung's arms.

Leung looked down at the girl and when she looked up he smiled broadly, as if to give her confidence.

"Now isn't that sweet?"

Leung swung forward to his knees and pushed Leen Forth behind him. He raised his gun toward the voice, but before he could squeeze the trigger, it was kicked out of his hand.

Arthur Grassione stood in the entrance to the shower stall.

"What do you think, I'm stupid? The first place you filthy gooks would hide would be in a shower."

Leung stood up to face the man. He looked

toward the gun but realized he would never reach it in time. Behind Grassione stood Big Vince Marino.

Leen Forth looked at the two men from between Leung's legs. Her face said nothing.

"Don't you think I know you Chinks'd stick together?" Grassione said.

Leung spat on Grassione's shoes. "Of course I think you're stupid," he said. "Because you are stupid. You're a stupid man getting stupider all the time."

Leung rose to his full height and walked toward Grassione, who gave way, then stepped aside and Big Vince Marino pushed a gun into Leung's forehead.

Leung stopped short.

"Stupid, huh?" Grassione said. "You were nothing but a gook fortune teller when I met you. And since then you been good for nothing more than taking out the garbage."

And because he was going to die and nothing would change that, Edward Leung let his anger give way to pity because he saw in a flash that came before his eyes that Grassione was going to die worse than he was.

"I told you," Leung said, "of death and dreams. Now you have your dream machine. Your death is following."

"Stuff it," said Grassione. Grassione bent down and picked up a large metal spike from the floor of the shower area. He walked very carefully up to Leung and with his left hand grabbed a handful of the man's black shiny hair and twisted.

Leung opened his mouth to scream but only a squeak came out. His eyes screwed shut in pain and his knees buckled. He felt Marino's gun jab into the back of his neck under his right ear.

Grassione's hand twisted harder. The pain coursed through Leung's body. His arms rose to the level of his shoulders, then swung down and his hands slapped the hard tile floor.

He was on his knees now, tears dripping across the bridge of his nose. His left ear touched the floor, the roar of silence filling it as his face was pressed down. His bent knees were kicked out from under him and he settled heavily onto his stomach. The hand was still twisted painfully in his hair, but all he really felt was the cold weight of the gun muzzle pressing under his right ear.

Grassione was on one knee, his face hard, his hand buried in moist hair, his knuckles white. Marino kept the automatic pushed against Leung's neck.

Grassione felt the weight of the iron spike in his hand.

Leung opened his eyes for the last time and stared at Leen Forth who huddled in the corner of the shower stall. He wanted to scream to her to run but his lips could form only the word "help." It came out in a soft whisper and his mouth stayed open. It was the last word he ever spoke.

Grassione drove the spike down into Leung's right ear.

The four inches of exposed steel under his clenched fist tore deep into Leung's head and his entire body jerked as all the brain's organic alarms and defenses rallied to that point.

Blood spurted out of the raw wound as Leung screamed and started to struggle.

Marino sat heavily on Leung's back, holding

the screaming man down. Grassione looked around, saw a hammer on the floor and lifted it up. As Leung uttered a last scream, Grassione brought the hammer down with all his strength onto the head of the spike.

The first swing drove the steel ram halfway through the brain. The second brought it to the left wall of the cranium, the skull cracking. The third connected the head to the locker room floor.

Grassione wiped his hands on Leung's suit, then stood up and wiped the sweat from his face with a monogrammed handkerchief.

He stood up and saw Leen Forth huddled in the corner of the shower stall.

Without a word, he moved his head sideways and Big Vince Marino left the room.

Still mopping his face, Grassione moved to where Leen Forth huddled and spun her around. He gave her one chance to scream, then stuffed his handkerchief deep into her throat.

He slapped her hard across the face, twice, threw her against the wall, and began to rip at the snap and zipper of her jeans.

For the first time since he'd boarded the boat, he heard the sound of the Muzak that was piped gently all over the yacht.

It was playing "Love Will Keep Us Together."

Chapter Eighteen

"I wish I knew where the girl was," Remo said.

"She is no longer on this rumpus," Chiun said.

"Campus. How do you know that?"

"She is on somebody's boat," Chiun said. "I know that because I am the Master."

"Yeah, but how do you really know?"

"The nice man with the television set said so."

"What nice man?"

"I don't know his name," Chiun said. "All those names sound alike."

"What boat is Leen Forth on?" Remo asked.

"Who knows? All boats look alike."

"You must have some idea," Remo said. He looked around at the trees that bordered the grassy field in front of Professor Wooley's house and wished that he were conducting this interrogation with a scarlet-crested titwillow. At least he could get an answer.

159

"Come on, Chiun, think," Remo said. "That little girl's life may be in danger."

"She is a Vietnamese," Chiun said. "A South Vietnamese at that. But never mind. I will do this for my country. She is on marshmallow's boat."

"Marshmallow?" Remo asked.

"Yes. Something like that."

"Massello?" Remo asked. "Was that the name? Massello?"

"Yes. Marshmallow. As I said. And another thing. She has the dream machine with her."

"The nice man told you," Remo said.

"Right."

"Was that nice man's name Grassione?" Remo asked.

"Yes. That was it."

"Chiun, that man is the leading contract killer for the crime syndicate in the United States."

"I knew there was something about him I liked."

It took Remo a telephone call to the local St. Louis Power Squadron to find out that Mr. S. Massello's yacht was docked in the Captain's Cove Marina in the southern part of the city, near Point Breese, and a few minutes later, in a car that might generously be called borrowed, they were zipping south along Route 55.

The gate to the boat yard was closed and bolted when Remo and Chiun arrived. The late afternoon sun was behind them and the Mississippi looked flat and black in its dying rays.

Chiun snapped the chain on the gate and he and Remo trotted quickly toward the back of the marina, when Remo saw the boat: *Il Avvocato*.

"It is strange to name a boat after a fruit," said Chiun.

"That's Italian for lawyer," Remo explained.

"And it is English for fruit," Chiun said. "Do not lie to me. I have not forgotten about electrical Washington."

The guard who had earlier been posted on the front gate had been pressed into service by Arthur Grassione after the "unfortunate accident" that had claimed the lives of Don Salvatore Massello and his two bodyguards, and now he patrolled the deck of the yacht with Big Vince Marino. The guard was the first to see Remo and Chiun as they came up the steps of the gangplank.

"Hold it," he called. "You can't come up here."

"Not even if I answer a riddle?" Remo said.

"Get out of here," the man said. He took his gun from a shoulder holster and waved it at Remo for emphasis. "G'wan. Beat it."

Remo nodded to Chiun who stood alongside him.

Just then Marino came around from the port side of the boat. "What's going on here?" he called.

"Trespassers, Vince," the other guard said.

Marion pulled his revolver and approached them at a lope. He stopped at the top of the gangplank and said, "What do you two want? Hey, it's the old guy with the television. What do you want?"

"Is this all of you?" Remo asked. "Are we all here?"

Marino pointed the gun at him in threatening

concentric circles that narrowed until the muzzle was fixed directly on Remo's stomach.

"You better beat it, pal."

"Just what I had in mind," Remo said. Without tensing his legs, he was airborne, moving toward the top of the gangplank. He clapped a hand over the young guard's face. The man fell back; his gun dropped helplessly to his side; he looked at Marino with two gaping cavities where his eyes had been, and then fell over the rail into the brackish waters of the river where he sank like a stone.

Marino tried to squeeze the trigger at Remo, but his finger wouldn't close on the ridged metal. The old Oriental had come up the gangplank and now his hand was around Marino's hand, and there was something wrong with the bones of Marino's hand, they wouldn't work anymore, and he looked down to see what was wrong, and he saw the old man's thin bony yellow hand close around the barrel of his gun and he saw the barrel bend toward the deck, as if it were made of summer tar.

"Where's the girl?" Remo said.

Marino shrugged.

"One more time," Remo said. "The girl."

"Dead. Dead. They're all dead," Marino gasped. The pain in his right hand where the old man held it was now radiating up his arm.

"Who killed her?" Remo asked.

"The boss," Marino gasped. "Grassione."

"You're not Grassione?" Remo said.

Marino shook his head vigorously. "No. No."

"You know what that makes you?" Remo asked.

162

"What?" Big Vince Marino gasped.

"Lucky. 'Cause you die fast."

He nodded to Chiun and then Marino felt the pain in his right hand, wrist and arm move upward to his shoulder. It spread outward, like the ripples of a rock in a stream, and when the small, almost gentle vibrations reached his heart, it stopped.

The man dropped heavily at Chiun's feet. Chiun looked down at him.

"What are you posing for?" Remo asked.

"Just basking in the excellence of technique," Chiun said.

"Well, bask around this boat and see if there are any more of these goons aboard. I'm going to look for Grassione."

"If you find him . . .".

"Yes," Remo said.

"Tell him thank you for lending me his television set today," Chiun said.

Chapter Nineteen

Arthur Grassione had the Dreamocizer on.

He was sitting in the downstairs lounge of the yacht, *Il Avvocato*, alone but for the bullet-shattered body of Don Salvatore Massello which lounged against the room's fireplace wall.

Grassione had used the telephone in the lounge to call Uncle Pietro in New York who had awarded his nephew warm congratulations on a job well done, and a promise that he, Pietro Scubisci, himself would call St. Louis now to inform people that Grassione had been working on the instructions of the national council and that any attack upon him would be regarded as an attack upon the national council itself.

"I got the machine too, Uncle," Grassione had said.

"What machine, nephew?"

"The television thing. They call it a Dreamocizer."

"Oh, that. Well, I do not watch much television anymore," Pietro Scubisci said. "Not since they take off the Montefuscos. That was a funny, that show. Like the old days with Mama and Pappa."

"Uncle, I think you should see this machine. I think we can make much money with it," Grassione said.

"How is that?" Scubisci asked quickly. "How is this different from the television set Cousin Eugenio got for me off the truck?"

And Grassione explained how Professor Wooley's Dreamocizer telecast a person's dreams, his wishes.

"You mean, I watch this television, I can see myself with lots of money, young again, with feet that don't hurt? Your aunt no longer has the boobies like two loaves of bread?"

"That's right, Uncle Pietro," Grassione said. "And it works for anybody. Whatever anybody wants, he can dream it on this machine."

"You be sure to bring this crazy machine home with you, Arthur," Scubisci said. "This I got to see. Me with hair, and feet that don't hurt." He laughed, a high tenor giggle.

"I will, Uncle, I will," said Grassione, but he hung up, not sure that his uncle had really grasped the significance of Professor Wooley's invention, the first major breakthrough in television since Grassione, as a boy, had first seen Felix the Cat at the 1939 World's Fair.

He remembered the demonstration that Wooley had given at the cafeteria. The little gook broad thinking about a Vietnam with no war.

166

Grassione had hooked up the Dreamocizer to the aerial connections of Don Massello's large console, and then had attached the electrodes as he had seen it done, two to his forehead, two to his neck.

He sat back in the soft leather chair in the room and thought of what he wanted to dream about.

He knew.

He wanted to dream about that bastard who had been going around the country, tearing up some of the organization's best people.

But he had trouble. All he could think of was Edward Leung's warning to him: "All life ends in dreams and death."

He shook his head to clear it of those thoughts. He was Arthur Grassione. He was on the trail of the man who was attacking the organization. He was going to find him and kill him. Destroy him.

Slowly the fuzzy image on the television set cleared.

He had first heard of this character on a drug run in New Jersey a few years ago. Then the presence had been felt after the organization almost became involved in a union dispute. Before the syndicate could influence anyone, the dispute was no more. Neither were most of the disputers.

Then there was that election in Miami. The papers were crying about a governmental kill squad, but nothing seemed to stop whoever it was who was wiping out the organization's men.

And finally again, just a short time before, with a famous Mafia home movie. Few had seen it and most of them were dead. It showed one dark-haired young man wipe out two teams of assassins. With his hands and nothing else.

Grassione had not seen the movie. He had been told though that the man was thin, with dark hair but had thick wrists, and moved fast.

There were more places that Grassione had felt the unknown man's movements vibrating through the mob.

And so now for sport, for relaxation, for relief, he was going to kill the man with the thick wrists.

The Sony TV showed a bright landscape. There was a man running across a field. He was a thin, dark-haired man. He had thick wrists. Grassione had seen him before. He knew it. But where?

Right. He had seen him run across the campus at Edgewood University.

The man kept running. Running.

Grassione had seen him somewhere else, too. Where? On television. Once before. Running in the Boston Marathon.

The man was running faster and faster now, but the ground around him was covered with a growing shadow. And then the man took one last step and a giant foot came down and squashed him like a hard-backed bug. Juicy.

Grassione laughed and clapped his hands together.

The picture suddenly changed. It was a romantic, dimly lit apartment. The dark-haired young man was sitting at a small round table, raising a glass of wine to a dark-haired beauty across from him. She was small and delicate, with Oriental eyes. The door of the room burst open and Grassione appeared with a submachine gun and opened fire.

Grassione watched and sat smugly in his chair aboard *Il Avvocato,* smiling his pleasure with himself.

The picture began to jump again. But instead of a new shot, the colorful landscape returned. Grassione frowned. The giant foot was still there, but it was slowly rising.

Grassione sat up and looked closer as the foot rose.

The shadow under the foot receded until the dark-haired man, now looking gentler than Grassione had pictured him, had lifted the foot an arm's length above him.

Grassione thought about the foot pressing down, crashing down on this peacefully smiling man with the thick wrists. Except the foot didn't. It began to crack.

The harder Grassione thought, the more cracks appeared and the wider they grew. Suddenly, the foot, as if made of plaster, crumbled around the young man's hands.

Grassione cursed and thought about himself machine-gunning this man, and the picture shifted back to the dimly lit apartment. Grassione was still firing the machine gun but the bullets were hitting nothing. They crashed into the table and the walls. The girl wasn't even there.

Grassione saw a blue shadow alongside his image on the television screen, and then his own machine gun was in his mouth and the bullets were smashing off the back of his skull, blood, brain, and bone flying off to color the walls.

Grassione shouted in spite of himself, twisting

in the leather chair. The picture lost the vertical, then the horizontal. Grassione tried to rise but could not.

A new scene came on the television. It was a devastated town street. A gray, dusty moonscape lined with craters and bullet holes. Sifting through the wreckage were dozens of Grassiones, all dressed in Nazi uniforms and carrying automatic rifles.

They would poke around a bit, then one would fire at a small animal, a rat, a shadow. They all seemed frightened.

The real Grassione sat sweating in his chair, riveted, wanting to rise but feeling unable to.

A wall fell down on the television screen atop several Grassiones. A human whirlwind hit the desolated town. The Nazi Grassiones started firing wildly. They succeeded in chipping wood and concrete as well as killing two more Grassiones, and then the blurry human form moved among the others, and where he moved, they died. Seemingly without touching them, he sent Grassiones flying all around him. His limbs were dark blurs and his head bobbed like a baloon in a cross current. He would seem trapped in the sights of a rifle, then the gun would be gone and his hand or foot would fill the television screen, then there would only be red.

Finally there was only one frightened Grassione left on the screen. He backed off slowly now from what finally had come into focus as a dark-haired young man with thick wrists. The television Grassione tried to run.

But the dark-haired man was on him, Grassione's head between his hand. With what looked like simple pressure, Grassione's head split open like a walnut shell.

Arthur Grassione screamed in his seat.

The picture wavered, then disappeared in a maze of vertical lines and a wash of red, then went black.

Grassione tried to get up. He tried to pull the electrodes off. But his hands couldn't reach his face. His head wouldn't move. He felt locked in the big soft leather chair.

Then a picture began to take shape before him. The dark television screen seemed to become a mirror. Grassione saw himself sitting in his chair with only one electrode on his temple and one on his neck. There were still four black wires coming from the Dreamocizer box on the back of the television set, but two of the wires were leading above him, over his chair.

Grassione concentrated on the screen. He bent a little so he could see better.

Standing behind the chair, arms crossed atop the back, was the thin, dark-haired man. He had thick wrists.

Grassione stared in wonder as the man reflected on the television set reached down to him.

He felt something on his chest.

He felt the pain.

He felt the air go out of him and his ribs crack and his heart pushed up against his spine. His blood vessels burst like popping corn, and his brain clouded, and he felt no more and saw and heard and did no more.

Remo let the two electrodes in his hand drop to Grassione's lap.

He sensed someone at the door and turned to see Chiun enter.

"There is no one else on this boat," Chiun said. "I found the girl. What he did to her was not nice."

"What I did to him wasn't much better, Little Father," said Remo.

He smiled at Chiun, then waved to the television set.

"Want to try it, Chiun?"

"A man should not come too close to his dreams," Chiun said.

"Oh, hogwash," Remo said. For the first time in days, he felt good. "Can't you just see it? Little hazel-eyed yellow men lusting after shining, black-haired almond-eyed beauties?"

"No," said Chiun.

"Of course you can. *Tales of Sinanju* starring Lad Lex. When we last left our story, Ming Hong Toy, playful research scientist and part-time song stylist, was about to marry Clark Wang Yu, gardener and part-time Godzilla impersonator, when her drunken father, Hing Wong, interrupted her joy with the news that her half-brother, Hong Kong, had been hit by a laundry truck while he was on a mercy mission, trying to smuggle soap back to the women of North Korea . . ."

"You are not funny," Chiun said. "You mock an old man's simple joys and you, yourself, go through life diminishing your skills by worrying about such things as home and duty and patriotism and country."

Remo recognized the hurt in Chiun's voice and said, "I'm sorry, Little Father."

"But who is the fool? Is it me with my moments of pleasure, my fantasies which I do not try to live? Or is it you, trying always to catch dreams you do not understand, and always failing?"

"Chiun, I'm sorry," Remo repeated, but Chiun had turned and left the cabin and all Remo's happiness of a few moments before had vanished in the wake of the hurt he knew he had caused the old man.

Later Remo went up on the deck and found Chiun leaning over the rail, staring across the wide Mississippi to the twinkling of lights from the other side of the river.

"Thinking of home, Little Father?"

"Yes," Chiun said. "It is like this on some nights. There are cool breezes and the water moves gently and as a boy I would stand on the shores and watch boats sail by and I would wonder where they were going and dreamed someday to go too."

"Now you've been to most places," Remo said.

"Yes. And none of them live up to the dreams I had in childhood. Dreams are like that."

Remo watched the lights of a passing boat twink on and off in signal to another boat.

"I'm going to call Smitty later tonight," Remo said. "I'm going to tell him to forget that house."

Chiun nodded. "That is wise, my son. You already have a home. I gave it to you as my ancestors gave it to me. Sinanju is your home."

Remo nodded.

"Not the village," Chiun said. "The village is just a dot on the map. But Sinanju itself. The art, the history, the science of all I have taught you, that is your home. Because that is what you are, and every man must live inside himself. That is every man's home."

Remo was silent.

Later, as he and Chiun started to leave the boat, Remo paused and went back aboard. Down in the lounge, he looked at the bodies of Grassione and Massello, men who had tried to live their dreams but had found that in death all men were the same, no matter what their dreams.

He walked toward the Dreamocizer thinking of all the people who had died in two days because one man had tried to harness dreams. He thought about Chiun. He thought about the house he would always want, but never again ask for, because men were kept alive by unfulfilled dreams. Dreams were to dream, not to realize.

Remo brought his arm up over the plastic box of the Dreamocizer.

"That's show biz, sweetheart," he said aloud.

He brought his arm down.

The Destroyer by Warren Murphy

Remo Williams is the perfect weapon—a cold, calculating death machine developed by CURE, the world's most secret crime-fighting organization. Together with his mentor, Chiun, the oriental martial arts wizard, The Destroyer makes the impossible missions possible.

Over 13 million copies sold!

☐	40-235-X	Created, The Destroyer	#1	$1.50
☐	40-276-7	Death Check	#2	1.50
☐	40-277-5	Chinese Puzzle	#3	1.50
☐	40-278-3	Mafia Fix	#4	1.50
☐	40-279-1	Dr. Quake	#5	1.50
☐	40-280-5	Death Therapy	#6	1.50
☐	40-281-3	Union Bust	#7	1.50
☐	40-282-1	Summit Chase	#8	1.50
☐	40-283-X	Murder's Shield	#9	1.50
☐	40-284-8	Terror Squad	#10	1.50
☐	40-285-6	Kill or Cure	#11	1.50
☐	40-286-4	Slave Safari	#12	1.50
☐	40-287-2	Acid Rock	#13	1.50
☐	40-288-0	Judgment Day	#14	1.50
☐	40-289-9	Murder Ward	#15	1.50
☐	40-290-2	Oil Slick	#16	1.50
☐	40-291-0	Last War Dance	#17	1.50
☐	40-292-9	Funny Money	#18	1.50
☐	40-293-7	Holy Terror	#19	1.50
☐	40-294-5	Assassins Play-Off	#20	1.50
☐	40-295-3	Deadly Seeds	#21	1.50
☐	40-296-1	Brain Drain	#22	1.50
☐	40-297-X	Child's Play	#23	1.50
☐	40-298-8	King's Curse	#24	1.50
☐	40-236-8	Sweet Dreams	#25	1.50
☐	40-251-1	In Enemy Hands	#26	1.50
☐	40-353-4	Last Temple	#27	1.50
☐	40-416-6	Ship of Death	#28	1.50
☐	40-342-9	Final Death	#29	1.50
☐	40-110-8	Mugger Blood	#30	1.50
☐	40-153-1	Head Man	#31	1.50
☐	40-154-X	Killer Chromosomes	#32	1.50
☐	40-155-8	Voodoo Die	#33	1.50
☐	40-156-6	Chained Reaction	#34	1.50
☐	40-157-4	Last Call	#35	1.50
☐	40-158-2	Power Play	#36	1.50

the EXECUTIONER by Don Pendleton

Over 22 million copies in print!

☐	40-027-9	Executioner's War Book		$1.50
☐	40-299-6	War Against the Mafia	#1	1.50
☐	40-300-3	Death Squad	#2	1.50
☐	40-301-1	Battle Mask	#3	1.50
☐	40-302-X	Miami Massacre	#4	1.50
☐	40-303-8	Continental Contract	#5	1.50
☐	40-304-6	Assault on Soho	#6	1.50
☐	40-305-4	Nightmare in New York	#7	1.50
☐	40-306-2	Chicago Wipeout	#8	1.50
☐	40-307-0	Vegas Vendetta	#9	1.50
☐	40-308-9	Caribbean Kill	#10	1.50
☐	40-309-7	California Hit	#11	1.50
☐	40-310-0	Boston Blitz	#12	1.50
☐	40-311-9	Washington I.O.U.	#13	1.50
☐	40-312-7	San Diego Siege	#14	1.50
☐	40-313-5	Panic in Philly	#15	1.50
☐	40-314-3	Sicilian Slaughter	#16	1.50
☐	40-237-6	Jersey Guns	#17	1.50
☐	40-315-1	Texas Storm	#18	1.50
☐	40-238-X	Detroit Deathwatch	#19	1.50
☐	40-238-4	New Orleans Knockout	#20	1.50
☐	40-317-8	Firebase Seattle	#21	1.50
☐	40-318-6	Hawaiian Hellground	#22	1.50
☐	40-319-4	St. Louis Showdown	#23	1.50
☐	40-239-2	Canadian Crisis	#24	1.50
☐	40-224-4	Colorado Kill-Zone	#25	1.50
☐	40-320-8	Acapulco Rampage	#26	1.50
☐	40-321-6	Dixie Convoy	#27	1.50
☐	40-225-2	Savage Fire	#28	1.50
☐	40-240-6	Command Strike	#29	1.50
☐	40-150-7	Cleveland Pipeline	#30	1.50
☐	40-166-3	Arizona Ambush	#31	1.50
☐	40-252-X	Tennessee Smash	#32	1.50
☐	40-333-X	Monday's Mob	#33	1.50
☐	40-334-8	Terrible Tuesday	#34	1.50

RICHARD BLADE by Jeffrey Lord

Richard Blade is Everyman, a mighty and intrepid hero exploring the hitherto-uncharted realm of worlds beyond our knowledge, in the best tradition of America's most popular heroic fantasy giants such as Tarzan, Doc Savage, and Conan.

Over 2.5 million copies in print!

☐	40-432-8	The Bronze Axe	#1	$1.50
☐	220593-8	Jade Warrior	#2	1.25
☐	40-433-6	Jewel of Tharn	#3	1.50
☐	40-434-4	Slave of Sarma	#4	1.50
☐	40-435-2	Liberator of Jedd	#5	1.50
☐	40-436-0	Monster of the Maze	#6	1.50
☐	40-437-9	Pearl of Patmos	#7	1.50
☐	40-438-7	Undying World	#8	1.50
☐	40-439-5	Kingdom of Royth	#9	1.50
☐	40-440-9	Ice Dragon	#10	1.50
☐	220474-1	Dimensions of Dreams	#11	1.25
☐	40-441-7	King of Zunga	#12	1.50
☐	220559-9	Golden Steed	#13	1.25
☐	220623-3	Temples of Ayocan	#14	1.25
☐	40-442-5	Towers of Melnon	#15	1.50
☐	220780-1	Crystal Seas	#16	1.25
☐	40-443-3	Mountains of Brega	#17	1.50
☐	220822-1	Warlords of Gaikon	#18	1.25
☐	220855-1	Looters of Tharn	#19	1.25
☐	220881-7	Guardian Coral Throne	#20	1.25
☐	40-257-0	Champion of the Gods	#21	1.50
☐	40-457-3	Forests of Gleor	#22	1.50
☐	40-263-5	Empire of Blood	#23	1.50
☐	40-260-0	Dragons of Englor	#24	1.50
☐	40-444-1	Torian Pearls	#25	1.50
☐	40-193-0	City of the Living Dead	#26	1.50
☐	40-205-8	Master of the Hashomi	#27	1.50
☐	40-206-6	Wizard of Rentoro	#28	1.50
☐	40-207-4	Treasure of the Stars	#29	1.50
☐	40-208-2	Dimension of Horror	#30	1.50

THE PENETRATOR
by Lionel Derrick

Mark Hardin is a warrior without uniform or rank, pledged to fight anyone on either side of the law who seeks to destroy the American way of life.

		Over 2 million copies in print!		
☐	40-101-2	Target is H	#1	$1.2
☐	40-102-0	Blood on the Strip	#2	1.2
☐	40-422-0	Capitol Hell	#3	1.5(
☐	40-423-9	Hijacking Manhattan	#4	1.5(
☐	40-424-7	Mardi Gras Massacre	#5	1.5(
☐	40-493-X	Tokyo Purple	#6	1.5(
☐	40-494-8	Baja Bandidos	#7	1.5(
☐	40-495-6	Northwest Contract	#8	1.5
☐	40-425-5	Dodge City Bombers	#9	1.5(
☐	220690-2	Hellbomb Flight	#10	1.2
☐	220728-0	Terror in Taos	#11	1.2
☐	220797-5	Bloody Boston	#12	1.2
☐	40-426-3	Dixie Death Squad	#13	1.5(
☐	40-427-1	Mankill Sport	#14	1.5(
☐	220882-5	Quebec Connection	#15	1.2
☐	220912-0	Deepsea Shootout	#16	1.2
☐	40-456-5	Demented Empire	#17	1.5(
☐	40-428-X	Countdown to Terror	#18	1.5(
☐	40-429-8	Panama Power Play	#19	1.5(
☐	40-258-9	Radiation Hit	#20	1.5(
☐	40-079-3	Supergun Mission	#21	1.2
☐	40-067-5	High Disaster	#22	1.5(
☐	40-085-3	Divine Death	#23	1.5(
☐	40-177-9	Cryogenic Nightmare	#24	1.5(
☐	40-178-7	Floating Death	#25	1.5(
☐	40-179-5	Mexican Brown	#26	1.5(
☐	40-180-9	Animal Game	#27	1.5(
☐	40-268-6	Skyhigh Betrayers	#28	1.5(
☐	40-269-4	Aryan Onslaught	#29	1.5(
☐	40-270-9	Computer Kill	#30	1.5(